A Light in the Storm

The Civil War Diary of Amelia Martin

BY KAREN HESSE

Scholastic Inc. New York

Fenwick Island, Delaware
1860

Gains for All Our Losses
by R. H. Stoddard

There are gains for all our losses —
  There are balms for all our pains;
But when youth, the dream, departs,
It takes something from our hearts,
  And never comes again.

We are stronger, and are better,
  Under manhood's sterner reign;
Still we feel that something sweet
Followed youth with flying feet,
  And will never come again.

Something beautiful is vanished,
  And we sigh for it in vain;
We behold it everywhere —
On the earth and in the air —
  But it never comes again.

Monday, December 24, 1860
Stormy. Wind N.E. Light.

I rowed across the Ditch this morning. Wish there were some other way to reach the mainland. Wind bit at my knuckles and stung my nose. Pulled hard at the oars to keep warm, landing Bayville beach in record time.

Bayville looked festive in its wreaths and ribbons and windows gold with candle glow.

Visited with Uncle Edward briefly. He has shaved off his beard! He looked so new with his whiskers gone, his chin so pale and tender. Beardless, he resembles Father less, but still enough. Even now, a stranger would know the two fair-haired men as brothers.

Uncle Edward slipped a package to me from under the counter. "Merry Christmas, Wickie," he said. "Open this tonight."

I hugged and thanked him, then handed over my present to him. He weighed it in his good hand, guessing.

It is *On the Origin of Species* by a man named Charles

Darwin. Mr. Warner recommended Darwin's book for Uncle Edward particularly.

At the confectionery, I purchased sweets for Father. Bought handkerchiefs for Keeper Dunne, and for William. Bought gloves for Grandmother.

But Mother's gift is best of all. I picked it up after finishing Grandmother's chores. Dear diary, let me tell you. Mother loathes the sea. Even though our rooms and the Lighthouse set back a good distance from shore, still we hear the waves breaking, the bell-buoy boat clanging. Mother longs to move back to the mainland, to Grandmother's cottage, away from Fenwick Island and the Light.

I expected Reenie O'Connell to do a good job. Day after day, she would arrive at the schoolhouse, her hands smudged with charcoal. But this afternoon, when I saw the finished drawing Reenie had made for Mother, it exceeded even my hopes. A charcoal window, captured in just a few strokes and smudges, the heavy hinged door, all in shadow, opening onto Commerce Street. "You have got the cottage just right," I told Reenie.

I paid her and brought the sketch to the Worthington house to show William, and to deliver his Christmas gift. All the Worthingtons approved of Reenie's sketch. Even Daniel.

William walked me back to the skiff. "Can you come skating with me and Daniel this week?"

I asked if the ice was thick enough for skating.

William grinned. "Not yet."

William! He is forever taking risks. That is how we became such good friends. Because of his risk taking.

It's almost nine now. Near the end of my watch. Father insists I take first watch. I don't mind. Sometimes the colors of the sunset paint the sky beyond the balcony of the Light. Then all the sea is awash with orange and dappled rose.

Only three hours more until midnight, until Christmas.

Father should be out to relieve me soon. The lamps are all burning well. The wind remains low. An occasional fit of rain slicks the glass surrounding the Light, but it is not a freezing rain and not too worrisome.

All the Christmas gifts are ready and waiting for tomorrow.

You, my diary, were in the package from Uncle Edward. Written upon the brown paper parcel, in Uncle Edward's peculiar script, was this note. *Open while you are on watch tonight, Wickie. You need a friend on the island. This might do.*

On the first page Uncle Edward has copied out a poem. It is a sad poem about gains and losses, about fleeting dreams, and the end of youth. I wonder why he chose to begin my diary with such a poem, but Uncle Edward is wise. Someday I will understand. My uncle knows me well. I do need a friend on Fenwick Island. You, dear diary, should do perfectly.

Tuesday, December 25, 1860
Stormy. Wind S.E. Moderate.

Christmas morning passed pleasantly. While Father, Keeper Dunne, and I cleaned the glass in the lantern room, Mother baked and made a good meal for us. Her happy presence in the kitchen cheered me mightily.

We gathered for Christmas dinner in the early afternoon, downstairs, in Keeper Dunne's quarters. Everything is dark there. Heavy draperies hang across his windows. Not even the light of the sea gets through. And Keeper Dunne looks just like his surroundings. Dark eyes droop at the same angle as his mustaches. But our Christmas was so pleasant, even Keeper Dunne smiled during our party.

Mother was at her best today. Sometimes she is waspish with Father. She can't seem to forgive him for landing us on this island off the coast of Delaware where the work never ends and the wind never ceases, where the sand is forever scratching at our skin and grinding between our teeth. Where nothing she plants survives the restless Atlantic and the ever-hungry water rats.

Keeper Dunne ignores the trouble between my parents. I try to do the same. I dream that things will be good again between them, the way they were before we came to live here, when Father commanded his own ship and came home to us at the cottage in Bayville, after months at sea. Mother and Father never fought then.

After our meal of pork, corn cakes, and beans, at last we opened Christmas gifts. Father gave me ribbons, one a dark, dark brown to match my hair, one the gray-green of the sea when it runs wild with spume. He also carved a model of our Lighthouse, hollowed out, so I might place a candle within its walls. I told him I loved his gifts and threw my arms around him.

Mother says that at fifteen I am too old to be so affectionate. When I am at school, assisting Mr. Warner, I try to behave as Mother says. But even then it is hard not to hug a child who has just read his own name for the first time.

Father has a way of smiling with his eyes when he is happy, and today his eyes were as gay as ever I can remember. "I'm pleased you like your gifts, Wickie," he said.

Though my Christian name is Amelia, Father has called

me Wickie for more than a year now, since he became Assistant Lightkeeper and we moved here to Fenwick Island. Wickie is a name of affection bestowed upon lightkeepers — I suppose because we are always tending the wicks. Mother hates to have me called so. She fears it will bind me to a lightkeeper's life. But I am already bound . . . in my heart and my soul, I am bound!

Mother handed me a small bundle. "Merry Christmas, Amelia," she said.

I opened her package to find two new aprons. What a sacrifice such a gift was for her. To sew when her hands and fingers often ache these days.

"Thank you, Mother," I said, coming over and kissing her dark hair. She blinked up at me, tears pooling in her eyes. "It is a wonderful gift," I told her. And I meant it.

Then I gave Mother Reenie's drawing of the cottage.

I could tell right away how very much she liked it. She sat in silence for several moments. Then, "Oh, Amelia, how lovely, how very, very lovely," and she would not let the little charcoal drawing out of her sight the rest of the afternoon. Father offered to fashion a frame for her and Mother thanked him, and there was a flicker of warmth between them in that moment that was for me the greatest gift of the entire day. If only the day could have ended then.

But we tarried by Keeper Dunne's fire. Father and I sang "Jingle Bells" and "Listen to the Mockingbird" and Mother and Keeper Dunne joined in. But then Father sang "The Old Gray Mare," the song used for Abraham Lincoln's campaign, though Father sang the original words, not the words about Lincoln coming out of the wilderness. And then he sang "Darling Nelly Gray," a song Mother abhors because of its abolitionist sentiment. Shortly after, Mother retired upstairs to our quarters, carrying Reenie's drawing. The spots on her cheeks told everything. She was angry at Father again, for bringing up the troubles so much on our minds these days.

Like Mother, I once believed unquestioningly in the institution of slavery. Then, a little over a year ago, a storm shipwrecked a family of fugitive slaves here on the island. That is when I first truly noticed the difference between my parents. Father wished to help the fugitives along to Philadelphia, to freedom. Mother insisted we turn them over to the authorities immediately, so they might be returned to their owner. You see, dear diary, Delaware is a border state. There are those here who oppose slavery, but there are also many who uphold it.

I remember rescuing the five limp, salt-streaked bodies clinging to their battered raft. A male, a female, and three bedraggled children. I had always thought Mother was right, that slaves were simpleminded. But these slaves, there was something in their eyes, in their way with one another, that made me question how simpleminded, in fact, they were. Still Mother insisted that getting them back home was the greatest kindness we could do them. Father disagreed. While they argued, our neighbor, Oda Lee Monkton, turned the fugitives over to the slave catchers and collected the reward.

Such a memory to recall on Christmas Day!

I left our rooms well before dark with a saucer of tasty bits for Napoleon. This past summer, Mother lost her entire garden to rats. I rowed to Bayville that very day and found Napoleon. He was a half-grown barn cat, then.

He is full grown now and worth his weight in gold. Our rat problem is greatly reduced. And he is my dearest companion on the island. Father and Keeper Dunne, too, find he makes for good company in the long, quiet hours on watch.

Napoleon ate the drippings and shreds of Christmas dinner eagerly, then scrubbed the saucer and himself, purring all the while. I stayed to play with him as long as I dared before running up the spiral stair to assist Father and Keeper Dunne in our nightly kindling of Fenwick Light.

Thursday, December 27, 1860
Fair. Wind S.W. High.
Inspection at 2:30 P.M. Condition very good.

No time to write yesterday. Today the Inspector from the Lighthouse Board came. He made no complaint against our work. He declared the Lighthouse trim and tidy, though he recommended a fresh coat of paint come spring. The salt, sand, and wind have been unusually hard on the buildings.

He was so pleased with our care of the station, remarking on the condition of the brass, on the polish of the glass. With his compliments coming so freely, he took us all by surprise at the very end of his inspection when he spoke unkindly of me.

He said Father and Keeper Dunne should alter their watches to eliminate the need for mine. He said I should not be standing watch over the Light. "She is little more than a child. And a female, at that. How can she make decisions in time of emergency?"

My temper sparked. How dare he question my ability? It is Father's opinion that in this year alone at least three men would have drowned but for my actions. I wear a scar across my cheek from rescuing William Worthington the September before last, when I was fourteen. Yet it would do me no good to show my anger to Inspector Howle.

Father defended me. He told Inspector Howle of my position as Assistant Teacher at the Bayville School. "She has been teaching two years," Father said. "If her work here at the Light does not demonstrate her reliability to you, contact Mr. Warner. Let him speak for her."

The Inspector looked into my face. I wished I could make the freckles across my nose disappear. Wished I could slim the lines of my cheeks, round as a baby's bottom.

Inspector Howle said if I was in service as an assistant teacher, then I must have enough to keep me occupied without the additional work of a Light station. How could I possibly get enough sleep standing five-hour watches?

"My work at school ends at one in the afternoon," I told him. "I am always back here in time to take first watch. I begin at four, finish at nine. I get by well."

The Inspector stared at Father disapprovingly. "You have raised your daughter to contradict a representative of the United States Lighthouse Board?"

Father put his hands on his hips and looked the Inspector directly in the eye. "I've raised my daughter to be honest, Inspector Howle. A quality the Board values highly, if I am not mistaken."

I do not overlook a single task, from the filling of the oil wells to the polishing of the doorknobs. Not a speck of dust do

I leave. There isn't a single situation for which the Light-keeping manual does not give step-by-step instructions, and since we came here nearly one and a half years ago, I have read from that manual as often as the tide has turned. If I drop oil on a lens, I clean it with spirits of wine. I know precisely how to trim a wick and adjust a flame. Precisely.

I don't ask for pay for my work. Nor even acknowledgment. I simply ask to be allowed to attend the Light. It is enough for me to know that by my actions, men are guided safely to port. I am good at my Lighthouse duties. I should continue.

When he left, Inspector Howle did not cite us for one single thing. Nor, in the end, did he instruct Keeper Dunne to relieve me of my watches.

So I am allowed to continue, unofficially, as assistant to the Assistant and Head Lightkeepers.

Inspector Howle shall see. In time I shall show the entire United States Lighthouse Board. I can keep the Light as well as anyone. And someday, I shall be given a Light of my own.

Friday, December 28, 1860
Clear. Wind N.W. High.

Cold has set in early. The millpond in Bayville is frozen over and William has started skating upon it, though I have yet to find time to join him.

A skin of ice borders the edges of Fenwick Ditch, making my daily trips to and from the mainland more difficult.

If the Ditch freezes fully over this winter, I shall walk across the water from island to mainland and back again. Mother would shackle me if she caught me. But wouldn't it be fine to do such a thing!

Crossed the Ditch this afternoon to pick up supplies in Bayville and see to Grandmother.

On my way to her cottage, I passed some men who were drinking in the street. One chased after me. I ran from him, my skirts hiked up. He didn't stand a chance of catching me. Even in my skirts and cloak I run faster than most boys. I thought first of running to Uncle Edward, but made Grandmother's in less time.

Didn't dare tell Grandmother what had happened. The man who had chased me came puffing past her window several minutes later, shouting drunkenly. He seemed already to have forgotten me. I asked if Grandmother knew the cause of the man's midday revelries.

Grandmother said three Negroes were hanged earlier today in the jail yard. At one o'clock. Just an hour before I passed.

After I did the washing up and the ironing, brought in wood and cleaned out the ashes, Grandmother asked me to sit and visit awhile. She asked after Mother. I told her about the inspection and how Mother and I received excellent scores on our housekeeping, and Father and Keeper Dunne and I on the accuracy of our logs.

Grandmother wanted to know if Father was treating Mother well.

I struggled to keep from losing my temper.

Grandmother said, "The captain of a vessel shall be not governed by his mate. But a married landsman shall." She said Father was not captain of his vessel anymore and he should remember that.

Grandmother is angry because Mother is too busy to come ashore often. But she is also still furious with Father. Five years ago, Father was stripped of command of his ship.

He knowingly broke the law by transporting north the leader of a slave rebellion. When the rebel slave was discovered on Father's ship, Father lost everything.

I was so young when it happened, only ten. But I remember feeling shame. I managed at last to put it out of mind. That's where it stayed until last year when we plucked the family of fugitive slaves from the sea and the whole question rose up again.

After washing up from tea, banking Grandmother's fire, and preparing a light meal for her dinner, I ran all the way to Uncle Edward's store. Uncle listened to my talk about the executed Negroes.

"That's the way it is here in Sussex County, Wickie."

Now, on watch, I remember again the fugitive slaves we rescued. Remember the expression on the children's faces as the slave catchers took them away.

Were they hanged, too?

Monday, December 31, 1860
Stormy. Wind S.W. Moderate.

Hard weather the last few days. No time to write. Today Napoleon followed me along the high tide line as I collected driftwood. Mother and Father argued again.

Napoleon keeps very close at my heels lately. He was waiting for me, outside the Lighthouse, when I came for my watch. Brought him up the stairs and dried his wet fur in my apron before Father and Keeper Dunne arrived to help me kindle the Light. This dark and stormy evening, I feel so deeply alone. Napoleon is even more a comfort in his own way than you, my diary, particularly as I read over the poem Uncle Edward placed in the beginning, particularly in view of the news he gave me today.

Uncle Edward heard that South Carolina voted to leave the Union! A state can't just stop being part of our country anytime it pleases!

Napoleon keeps nosing under my hand as I write, making me smudge my letters. He is purring and needling my lap with his claws. Outside the storm blows, whistling around the Lighthouse. The tower sways, buffeted by high winds. But Napoleon, at least, is happy for the moment.

I wish I could be happy. I wish Uncle Edward was wrong about South Carolina. But Uncle Edward is seldom wrong about anything.

Thursday, January 3, 1861
Rain and Fog. Wind S.W. Fresh.

Won't make excuses. Some days I simply cannot write. Enough said.

This morning, Father and I left the station at 9 A.M., heading for Frankford on our big expedition to buy monthly supplies of flour, sugar, coffee, and the like.

In Frankford, the talk was everywhere about South Carolina. It alarmed me to hear the pleasure taken by so many at the idea of secession. Our country's history has been my fascination since I was small. I know at what sacrifice our nation was born. To consider undoing the country over the issue of slavery and where it shall be permitted is unthinkable.

Saw Mr. Warner in Frankford. At least he spoke of something other than secession. He spoke of the new school term beginning next week. "I've heard from several parents that their children miss you," Mr. Warner said. "And I miss you too, Miss Martin. Did your uncle like his book?"

I told him how much Uncle Edward was enjoying Darwin. Mr. Warner said he had a book for me to read. *Fifteen Decisive Battles of the World* by Edward Shepherd Creasy. I shall have it when school resumes.

I am eager to return to my post as Assistant Teacher at the Bayville School. I miss the children very much.

Father and I returned across the Ditch just in time for my watch. Keeper Dunne had already begun preparations to kindle the Light. Because we returned from Frankford so late, I missed dinner. Father brought a basket from Mother out to me. I listened, with pleasure, to his steady steps climbing the spiral stair.

Now, with Father back at the house, sleeping, I eat my cold pork and biscuits, alone, gazing out to sea. As the light sweeps across the dark, I strain my eyes, watching. I have just you, my diary, for company tonight. And I'm afraid I have made a grease stain on you.

Monday, January 7, 1861
Clear. Wind S.E. Moderate.

Helped Mother with breakfast chores, then joined Father and Keeper Dunne in the Light. Cleaned soot from the lantern, trimmed wicks, and polished brasswork before heading across the Ditch for school.

The current swept me down channel, but finally I made my way across.

Reenie O'Connell and my young Osbourne scholars joined me on the path. Bayville School is not much to look at. A low, unpainted building furnished with double seats, a single blackboard, a woodstove, and Mr. Warner's desk. The boys tend the woodstove, each bringing a stick with them in the morning. Even little Jacky Osbourne carries a chunk of firewood for the stove.

I wish I could speak with someone at school about all the matters troubling me. William is no longer a student. Both he *and* Daniel work now. But even if William came to school, lately, as I question slavery more and more, William gets thorny with me and I with him.

I wish I could speak with Reenie, but I can't. Reenie's father sides with the secessionists. Her family has no love for Abraham Lincoln.

Today I began my third year as pupil teacher, assisting Mr. Warner. Mr. Warner says I should continue my studies at the University next year. He says I would make a very good teacher.

I haven't mentioned Mr. Warner's idea to Father or Mother. I'd very much like the opportunity to learn more about history and teaching, but I have no wish to leave Fenwick Island.

After school, I took care of Grandmother's chores. She has begun making a list for me each day and the lists get longer and longer with every visit. It's confounding. She generally can't abide having me in the same room. I'm a big and muscled girl, not at all the dainty lady she'd wished for in a granddaughter.

I finally broke free of Grandmother and visited Uncle Edward but I had only a few minutes before heading back to the Light. We discussed Mr. Darwin's book and I showed Uncle the *Fifteen Decisive Battles* from Mr. Warner.

I felt I must talk with Uncle Edward and give voice to the trouble in my heart.

Uncle called for Daisy to look after things and took me aside. Last year, Daisy was Reenie O'Connell's house slave. Uncle Edward bought her from the O'Connells, then freed her. Daisy stayed on to work for Uncle Edward. She could go as a free woman wherever she pleased, but she pleased to stay at Uncle Edward's store, sleeping downstairs in a room she fixed herself.

Uncle Edward frowned under his smart mustaches. "What is it, Wickie?"

"South Carolina leaving the Union," I told him. "I'm frightened."

Uncle Edward's eyes showed understanding.

"I'm a little frightened, too, Amelia."

He stretched his good hand over the top of mine. His withered hand hung at his side.

I stopped at the church for one moment before rowing home. The ropes of evergreens from Christmas still hang along the galleries. Knelt and prayed, for the preservation of our country and for the preservation of my parents' marriage.

And now I stand watch. I've been tracking the lights from

a small ship heading south. Have made note of its progress in the log.

I wonder if there are any corn cakes left from dinner. I am hungry.

Thursday, January 10, 1861
Clear. Wind N. W. Moderate.

Oh, my diary, Uncle Edward gave me the most horrible news today. Three drowning deaths. Children venturing on ice not thick enough to support their weight. The first two deaths were my scholars, Winfield Pearce, six years old, and John Moore, eight. The boys died last night, together. I knew of *their* deaths already, before Uncle Edward told me. Children at school could speak of nothing else. The boys fell through the ice at Churchman's Pond. I am bereft to lose those little boys.

Yet, the third death Uncle Edward revealed to me tore truly through my heart. William Worthington, my William, drowned in Sharp's Millpond last night.

I couldn't believe it when he first told me. Surely if such a thing had happened I would have known.

"William was skating at the head of the pond," Uncle Edward said. "He ventured too far out, where the ice was still thin. He broke through and drowned before Daniel could reach him. I'm sorry, Amelia. I know you were friends."

Friends! Oh, much more than friends.

I sat with Uncle Edward. I could only think of the way William unwrapped his bread from its cloth before he ate, and the smell of the woods the day we went out gathering chestnuts, and how William's eyes widened when I told him about storms at the Lighthouse. How we argued about stupid things. How alive he was. Oh, how will it be without William?

Uncle put his arm around my shoulder.

"I should go see Mrs. Worthington, and Daniel, and the little girls." But I couldn't make myself move.

William had asked me to come skating with him. If I had been there he would still be alive. I would have kept him from the thin ice, I would have kept him from falling through. But even as I thought it, I knew it wasn't true. William was stubborn. He went where he pleased. I couldn't have stopped him any more than Daniel could have.

Uncle Edward said, "Wickie, we should take a holiday. Just the two of us. Professor Armes is speaking in Smyrna this weekend." I tried paying attention but I could only think of William.

I told Uncle Edward no. I could not leave my school

chores, I could not leave my Light chores. I could not walk away from William Worthington.

I rowed back to the island. Napoleon greeted me as I pulled the skiff to the boathouse. I walked along the strand, holding Napoleon against me.

Oda Lee Monkton appeared suddenly on the beach, her arms crossed at her chest, her short hair sun-streaked and wind-tossed. I was close enough to see the puffiness under her eyes, her face with its four deep lines, two connecting her nose to her mouth, two connecting her mouth to her chin. She was close enough to see my tear-streaked face.

Napoleon, startled by Oda Lee's sudden appearance, paddled free of my arms and ran through the dune grass.

I ran, too.

Back to the house. I found Mother upstairs, sewing in the front room, a blanket over her lap, her long hair spilling across her shoulders. Father sat carving in his corner.

"What is it, Amelia?" Mother asked the moment she saw me. "What's wrong?"

I was too upset to talk.

"Come with me," she said.

I followed her to her bedroom. She lightly touched my face. It was enough to open the door on my sorrow.

When I returned to the front room, Father was preparing to take my watch. "I can manage," I told him. We headed down together.

Light spilled pink across our faces, the pink of sunset. Wrapping my cloak around my shoulders, I raised my hood for the short walk to the Light. Father and I climbed the Lighthouse steps together, joining Keeper Dunne in the lantern room, where we lit the wicks. Keeper Dunne pulled the chain until it hung at its longest, down through the center of the stairs, then started the clockwork. The heavy Light began to turn, floating on its greased base.

As if this were any night, the Light began its nightly circle of darkness and flash.

Keeper Dunne returned to the house. Father and I descended one flight below, to the watchroom. We stepped onto the balcony, the wind snapping at our cloaks. In the twilight, we watched a ship steam past several miles out. No doubt the captain took comfort in the flash of our Light.

Father nodded to the distant ship. "Safe passage," he whispered.

I thought of William. Safe passage, I prayed.

Friday, January 11, 1861
Rain. Wind N.E. Light.

Buried William Worthington.

Thursday, January 17, 1861
Cloudy. Wind N.W. Moderate.

Visited Uncle Edward after school. There was an earthquake in South Carolina! The quake sent people running into the streets. They thought their houses were falling down.

Uncle Edward said their houses *were* falling down, from a different kind of earthquake altogether. "For pity's sake, the very house of America is falling down because of their actions."

Mr. O'Connell was in Uncle Edward's store testing the weight of hoes, close enough to hear Uncle Edward's words. Mr. O'Connell still treats Daisy like a slave. She works in back when Reenie's father comes in. After hearing us speak out against South Carolina, Mr. O'Connell pitched the hoe he'd been favoring back against the wall. He left without buying a thing.

This afternoon, the wind pulled at my cloak as I made the quick passage from our quarters to the Lighthouse. I left for the Light early, to keep from hearing my parents argue. I can no longer stop them, no matter how I try.

Keeper Dunne was first to join me in the lantern room. He has been looking gray lately, gray smudges under his eyes, gray smudges under his cheekbones. I fear he is ill.

Father joined us moments later.

"Shall Father and I take your watch tonight?" I asked.

Keeper Dunne shook his head no. "Just need some rest, I think."

Father guided him toward the head of the stairs, offering again to stand double watch as Keeper Dunne prepared to descend.

"No thank you, John," Keeper Dunne said. "I'll leave you two to kindle the Light, though. Just see I'm awake before you go to bed, Amelia." And he climbed slowly down the stairs, his steps ringing like a dull bell.

As we lit the wicks, I spoke almost in a whisper. "Father, it feels as if the world is coming to pieces."

Father harrumphed.

I looked down on our house through the lantern glass. Mother used to stand and watch us kindle the lights as night fell. Tonight there was no sign of Mother.

Saturday, January 19, 1861
Clear. Wind N.W. Moderate.

Mother nearly burned the house down last evening, though she doesn't know it. Father was in the lantern room; he'd come early to relieve me. When I returned to the house, I smelled smoke. Mother had washed my extra stockings for me and hung them by the fire before retiring for the evening. By the time I reached them, my stockings were ablaze. Throwing water on the fire, I put it out quickly. Except for ruined stockings, a scorched fire-board, and a lightly toasted arm, all is well. Another five minutes and we might have lost everything.

Today Mother said she kept smelling smoke. To settle her mind, Keeper Dunne promised he would write the Lighthouse Board and request a visit from the chimney sweep as soon as could be arranged.

Mother insisted we not wait. That we must clean the chimney ourselves.

Father surprised me by agreeing to Mother's demand. He must still care for her. Why else would he spare her feelings by hiding the truth . . . that she, not the chimney, had caused the house to smell of smoke.

Tomorrow, though it is the Sabbath, we shall tie several stones onto ropes, climb to the roof, and let the ropes down the chimney, raising and lowering the stones until the worst of the black crisps of soot are scraped off the chimney's inside walls. We shall have twice the mess to clean when we finish, but Mother should be satisfied.

I wish I could help her somehow. Her moods rise and fall with the pain in her joints, with the battles with Father. Most of the time she simply seems sad. As if she finds no beauty, no joy in this life. How can she live in such a place and not see its beauty?

I love Mother. I want her to feel gay again. To laugh. To be content. But she seems determined to be unhappy with Father and with our position at the Light. I should not say this, and I could not say this to anyone but you, my diary, not even to Uncle Edward, but there are days when I am angry at Mother. Because she is so blind to Father's goodness, because she hates the Light and the sea.

Sometimes, what I write here is all that keeps me calm. Putting the tumble of anger and fear down on paper gives me power over it. Then I don't feel so helpless.

I record the wind, the weather, the ship sightings in the Keeper's log, but here, in my own diary, I write all the rest.

Sunday, January 20, 1861
Clear. Wind N.E. to S.E. Light.

Keeper Dunne led us in prayer this morning. We have reached the lowest point of cold so far this winter, the thermometer standing at 4 degrees.

We cleaned the chimney this afternoon.

No more time to write. The oil congeals and will not pour. I must warm it before I can refill the wells that feed the Light.

Monday, January 21, 1861
Cloudy. Wind S.E. Light.

The sudden rising of the temperature brought relief, even to Mother, who spent the day doing wash.

The only relief it has not brought is to Mr. O'Connell's bad humor. Reenie's father has forbidden her from talking with me. This latest outburst, I fear, comes from his presence in Uncle Edward's store the other day when we were discussing South Carolina. At first Mr. O'Connell threatened to withdraw Reenie from school. But she spent the weekend calming him. She promised she would not listen to any talk of Abolition, from anyone. And in particular she would have no conversations with me. She explained everything to me this morning, quickly, without looking at me once, before she slipped to the back of the procession of Osbournes.

As soon as I returned home from Bayville this afternoon, I worked beside Mother. She had such energy. Her humor was so good. Her knuckles were hardly swollen.

I dare to hope she is recovering and all will be well from now on.

Thursday, January 24, 1861
Clear. Wind S.E. Moderate.

Father and I made the mistake of discussing politics within Mother's earshot.

She colored and grew angry. "I will not listen to this talk," she snapped. Without looking back at us, she retreated to her room.

I heard her weeping. Father heard her, too.

A little later, when she grew quiet, I went in to her. She was sitting at her dressing table, gazing at the charcoal drawing of the cottage, which Father has not yet framed for her. I promised I'd row her to the mainland to visit Grandmother this weekend.

"Thank you, Amelia," she said.

I am heavyhearted. How could Father and I have made such a mistake, when Mother was doing so well?

Tuesday, January 29, 1861
Cloudy and Snow. Wind S. W. Moderate.

A covering of snow has transformed Bayville into a soft, white plain, but here, on the island, the wind blows the snow away before it has a chance to settle. Just now, for the second time on my watch, I have had to inch up the ladder onto the narrow balcony that runs around the outside rim of the Light. The wind blew strong enough to rattle the ladder so that it shifted in the buffeting gusts, even with my weight upon it. Clinging with one hand to the slick balcony rail, I scraped ice and snow from the glass, keeping my eyes averted so as not to be blinded by the flash. Below and beyond, the sea thunders, the wind howls, and the snow has scoured my cheeks and hands with its stinging pins. Clearing ice off the outside of the lantern glass is dangerous; it is the chore that most frightens me. I would rather take on a rescue on the stormy sea than face the ice-slick ladder and the beastly wind.

I hope the glass does not ice up again tonight.

Thursday, January 31, 1861
P. Cloudy. Wind N.W. Light.
Received a delivery of whale oil.

Uncle Edward and I sat quietly in the afternoon and gazed out
at the patches of snow remaining from the storm two days
ago. I stopped at the Worthingtons' before coming to Uncle's.
Mrs. Worthington seems to find me too much a reminder of
William. I fear my visit made her grief more difficult to bear.
Daniel avoids me entirely. Only the little girls seemed pleased
when I came. Perhaps I should not visit soon again.

Uncle told me that the states of South Carolina and
Mississippi have ordered all their residents to pay a $12 prop-
erty tax on the head of each and every slave. The rebels figure
that's the best way to raise money to run their new country.

A $12 tax on every slave!

I don't dare tell Father what else Uncle Edward told me.
Uncle and I actually laughed over it, but I'm not certain Father
would find it funny. It seems the Delaware senate, in an effort
to settle down our hotly divided state, has proposed intermarriage between Southerners and Northerners to hold the Union
together. That is what my mother and father have, a marriage
between South and North; she from Sussex, the southernmost
county in Delaware, and Father from up north in New Castle.

They might as well be from Charleston and Boston, as different as they stand on the issues of slavery and secession. All I can think is the Government had better have another plan in mind, because I do not think this intermarriage idea is going to work.

The paper Uncle Edward read from says now Georgia has seceded from the United States. Dear Lord, if you add Georgia to South Carolina, Mississippi, Florida, and Alabama, we have five states now that have left the Union!

Thursday, February 7, 1861
Cloudy. Wind N.W. Moderate.

A flock of birds hit the glass last night. It must be over four months since the last time. They are blinded by our Light and crash into the lantern room. I hate cleaning up their bodies afterward; all frozen stiff, their necks broken. The dead birds were everywhere this morning, strewn over the ground, piled on the Lighthouse balconies. I discovered a crack in the lantern room glass on the seaward side before I left for school. Reading through the log tonight, I see that Keeper Dunne has made a report. Someone from the Lighthouse Board will come to inspect the damage soon. I hope it won't be Inspector Howle.

We must get the station sparkling before the Inspector comes. Mother did the scrubbing today while I was at school. She could barely get down on her knees, barely hold the brush when I bid her good-bye this morning. But she worked all day anyway, in spite of the pain in her hands and her knees.

Tonight, though, after my watch, I must retrace Mother's footsteps and clean all the places she missed because, for the first time, she did not scrub well enough to pass inspection.

Friday, February 8, 1861
Cloudy and Rain. Wind S.E. Light.

Temperature in the fifties.

Saturday, February 9, 1861
Stormy. Wind N.W. Light.

Temperature within one degree of zero this morning.

Monday, February 11, 1861
Clear. Wind W.N.W. Light.

Temperature up around sixty.

Chill again. This restless weather is much like Mother's moods, high and low, and never a clue as to what each day might bring.

After morning chores I rowed across the Ditch and walked to school with the Osbourne children at my heels. Reenie, good to her word, maintained a safe distance behind.

I miss William Worthington. I see Daniel in passing. He is two years older than I. Daniel has taken his brother's death hard. Perhaps if we spoke together of William, it would bring comfort to us both.

I did the marketing for Grandmother, filling her cupboards. Grandmother sat in her hearth chair, a blanket up around her neck. She crossed her arms under the blanket and cursed Mr. Lincoln. The bones of her elbows poked inside the blanket like a pair of fishhooks.

The name of our President-Elect enters most conversations these days. Down here in Sussex County, the comments are mostly unkind.

In the paper, Lincoln's route to Washington was mapped out for all to see. "He won't be traveling any straight lines,"

Grandmother said. "Probably run the Government just as crooked."

I banked her fire, wished her good day, and stepped into the fog.

No time for Uncle Edward. Rowing home across the Ditch, I tensed against the tide. The current in the channel was stronger than usual. The current inside me, too.

The paper says that down south, in Montgomery, Alabama, the Confederates have elected Jefferson Davis as President of their "country." They declare a new President and Mr. Lincoln isn't even to Washington yet.

Friday, February 15, 1861
Cloudy. Wind N.E. Fresh.
Inspection. The cracked glass must be replaced.

The air has turned as mild as mid-April. Got my young scholars to point out the spring birds: the robin, the black-bird — children and birds, all chattered away as merrily as if they believed spring really had come. I am delighted with the sight of a single robin. Grandmother said she saw one under her fence and heard it chirping through the closed window. There are no robins at the Lighthouse yet.

I promised to row Mother across next Sunday so she might attend services with Grandmother and see Grandmother's robin with her own eyes.

Wednesday, February 20, 1861
Fair to Rain. Wind E. to N.E. Fresh.

Opened the windows, even in the Lighthouse, before leaving for Bayville this morning, hoping the warm breeze would freshen the stale winter air in our rooms.

But the sun disappeared midmorning. As I rowed back home across the Ditch, the station took on an eerie light. Rain began, with the wind driving the downpour like an attack of spears.

I ran to the house, up to Mother's room to help her with the windows, and found her facing out to sea. She was wet with rain and salt spray, her hair and her gown blowing wildly about her frame. Paper, hair combs, and silks tumbled about the room.

"Mother, what is it?" I asked.

"Amelia," she cried. "I will go mad with the din of that bell. Stop it, please! Stop it." Mother cried for the pain in her head.

I fashioned cloths in a muff to protect her ears.

Closing her windows, I remained long enough to see Mother wrap herself in a dry gown. Reenie O'Connell's drawing of Grandmother's cottage was under Mother's dressing table, water-spotted and curled with the damp.

Made haste down to the cellar to lift the boulders onto the lid of the cistern. It is my duty to keep the sea out of our supply of fresh water.

Closing windows along the way, I rushed round and round, up the Lighthouse stairs. Though it was still early, the sky had darkened to where the Light needed kindling.

Father, Keeper Dunne, and I pulled away the protective curtains, trimmed the wicks in the fourteen lamps, filled the wells, and lit the Light.

We had not finished when the storm hit full force.

As I squinted into the gloom, a gull blew past, beating its wings, struggling to stay aloft. The bell-buoy boat clanged at its mooring just offshore. Poor Mother.

But thank goodness for the din. I pray sailors will hear the clanging above the scream of the storm, for I don't know how far the Light can reach through this weather.

Can't sit still. The storm has caused a restlessness in my mood. Even in this diary I write in fits and starts, checking the Light, trying to peer through the storm to the sea, watchful for ships, watchful for danger.

Quickly I must put you away, my diary. There is the sound of footsteps on the stair. I hope it is Father coming to stand watch with me.

I have been listening, waiting, for half an hour. No one has come. I keep waiting for someone to appear. But no one comes.

My hair stands up on my spine. Perhaps a ship has gone down and the ghost of a sailor has come to haunt me because the Light did not show brightly enough, the bell did not clang loudly enough, to save him.

Thursday, February 21, 1861
P. Cloudy. Wind N.W. High.

I looked around the island this morning for something, anything, that might explain the footsteps I heard last night in the Lighthouse, but I saw nothing out of the ordinary. I am grateful the footsteps have not come again tonight.

Mother's head was still pounding this morning. I consulted with Father and Keeper Dunne. It was decided I should leave early and stop at Dr. McCabe's before going on to school.

Told Dr. McCabe about Mother. Told him about her swollen joints and her head.

He asked if there wasn't a certain time of day harder on Mother than others.

Morning, I told him. The worst is always morning.

While Dr. McCabe made a powder for Mother, he asked my age.

"Sixteen in May, sir."

We talked about the Lighthouse chores, about school, and such.

"And you look after your grandmother, too, don't you?"

Dr. McCabe suggested we give Mother a vacation from the Light and let her remain awhile on the mainland. He thought perhaps she might stay briefly at the hospital in Frankford.

"Is she so sick?" I asked.

Dr. McCabe said he'd like to examine her first but he thought Mother's joint problems might benefit from additional medical attention.

Finished *Fifteen Decisive Battles* and returned it to Mr. Warner. He pulled *A Chronological History of the United States* from his desk and handed it to me.

I was no good in classes today, worrying about Mother.

Mr. Warner noticed I was not myself. "Where is that fine, sharp mind today, Miss Martin?" he asked, tapping his own head. He asked if I wished to leave early, and I did.

Uncle Edward told me not to fret over Mother.

I noticed a lack of customers in Uncle's store.

He explained that some of his neighbors had stopped coming to make purchases there. He has the national flag flying and Daisy, after all.

When I asked how many customers he'd lost, Uncle Edward said, "Most.

"Funny, isn't it. I have no business, while up in Connecticut, Colonel Colt's pistol factory is running day and night."

I lifted a jar, dusted it, dusted the shelf beneath it, then put the jar back down. I needn't have bothered. Daisy keeps the shop spotless.

Now I am in the third hour of my watch. Mother was grateful for the powder from Dr. McCabe, and when I left her to come on watch, she was resting comfortably. Father and Keeper Dunne made repairs on the bell-buoy boat, which suffered a leak during Wednesday's storm. Everyone agrees they must get the bell back in commission as quickly as possible. Everyone but Mother, that is. Mother would just as soon the boat broke its mooring and sailed away, or sank to the bottom of the sea. Mother says the bell ship is like a tethered whale with a gong in its gullet.

But to me the bell is a good and comforting sound.

Tonight I can hear music. It is eerie and beautiful. I have heard it before. It comes to me on the wind. I don't know if it is really music or just a trick played by the sea. If it is a trick, it is a very good trick, indeed.

Wednesday, February 27, 1861
Clear. Wind W. Fresh.

What a beautiful day. The mild weather calls forth the caroling of birds. In Bayville, the blooming faces and bright eyes of my young scholars swell my heart with joy.

It is hard to be without hope when the weather is so kind. Even the sea seems at peace.

Thursday, February 28, 1861
P. Cloudy. Wind N.W. Fresh.

Mr. Lincoln has arrived at last in Washington. He took the final leg of his trip secretly, by carriage, because of threats on his life.

In one week, he inherits the trouble of this great, unhappy country. In one week, the responsibility will be his — whether we come together again as a Union, or fall entirely to pieces. And here we sit, in Delaware, on the border between North and South, half the state holding slaves, half the state opposed to the practice. I do not envy our President-Elect. It is hard enough to hold a family together. Poor Mr. Lincoln. It is in his hands to hold a whole country together or watch it fall apart. My hands are calloused and strong from rowing and working the ropes, from lifting and carrying barrels of oil and scrubbing stone floors and spiral stairs, but I do not know if they are strong enough to hold Mother and Father together.

Mr. Lincoln's hands . . . they must be a thousand times stronger than mine. Please God, give Mr. Lincoln strong hands.

Monday, March 4, 1861
Fair. Wind N. Fresh.

The weather is rare indeed for the season and would have done credit to May or June; in fact, yesterday and today the thermometer rose to 80 degrees — 4 degrees above the average summer heat. The consequence is the blooming out of crocus and other early spring flowers, and a general bursting of the buds and spreading of leaf everywhere, even here on Fenwick Island.

Mother hummed today as she washed.

Thursday, March 7, 1861
Cloudy. Wind N.E. Fresh.

Now we can say *President* Lincoln, for his presidency is official as of Monday last. I wish him good luck.

Our new President says the Union is not broken. He says this issue is a matter of law, and he shall see to it that the law is faithfully followed.

Mother despises President Lincoln. Father and I sat with her this afternoon as she prepared dinner. I read her articles from the paper that promise our President will not interfere with the practice of slaveholding in the Southern states, nor obstruct the return of fugitive slaves. But she would not listen.

"He will have the whole country overrun with colored," she said. "You just wait. How can anyone trust a man so ugly?"

Father turned red. "Damn you, woman. You judge everything by appearance!"

My cheeks burned.

Father's fury mounted. "If the Negro seems stupid it is because he has not been given the opportunity to learn. The fact that so many Negroes can read and write and handle themselves in this world is a testament to how great they might be."

"Do not speak this rubbish to me," Mother screamed.

I stood between them. Helpless.

Friday, March 8, 1861
Fair. Wind S.E. Fresh.

Before I left Bayville this afternoon, Uncle Edward offered to treat me to ice cream from the confectionery. I caught sight of William Worthington's mother as we crossed the street. I ran to inquire after her health, and to see the little girls, and have news of Daniel. Mrs. Worthington took me in her arms and held me. Her hand stroked my hair. "How I have missed you, Amelia," she whispered in my ear.

Oh, Mrs. Worthington, I have missed you, too.

Thursday, March 14, 1861
Cloudy and Rain. Wind N.E. Fresh.

Father and I took Beans and the wagon across the Ditch while the weather was still balmy. We rode to Frankford for supplies.

In Frankford we heard politics discussed everywhere.

Perhaps this sounds strange, dear diary, but I am growing used to it all. At the Lighthouse, we go on, performing chore after chore. We trim and light the wicks, opening each mantle, adjusting the height of each flame, swinging the doors shut, and fastening the catches. We wind the clockwork of the lantern carriage. We watch through the night, ensuring that the beacon stays lit. And at dawn we extinguish the Light. This is the only way I know to go on.

Perhaps it is because of the constancy of the Light that my heart can grow used to the uncertainty of everything else.

Tuesday, March 19, 1861
Cloudy and Rain. Wind S.E. Moderate.

Caught a shad.

Caught sight of Oda Lee Monkton, too, while fishing out in the skiff.

Oda Lee's husband deserted her years ago. He went to sea and never returned. Since then she has kept to herself, living on what she can scavenge. She would prefer for us to fail in our duty of keeping the good Light; she lives at cross-purposes, waiting only for ships to founder on the sandbars and shoals.

Oda Lee lives off wrecks. She has become a pirate. And she keeps company with slave catchers.

Keeper Dunne calls Oda Lee "the mooncusser." When the moon shines, a ship is far less likely to run aground. So people who make their livelihood from scavenging wrecks curse the moonlit nights.

Mother forbids me to have anything to do with Oda Lee, and on this matter I have no difficulty complying.

Thursday, March 21, 1861
Clear. Wind N.W. Fresh.

Last night the millponds froze over to the thickness of an inch — the thermometer being at 11 degrees this morning. I fear the peaches on the mainland are destroyed.

Tonight I am so tired. Must force my eyes to stay open, force myself to remain alert. If I let the Light go out, even for a moment. . . . Reenie O'Connell said once she would never want such responsibility. She said it was hard enough to look after a family, how much more difficult to look after the sea and those who sail upon it. But it doesn't seem difficult to me. Except when I am so tired.

Keeper Dunne led us in morning prayer.

Dr. McCabe came out later and stayed for the noon meal, complimenting me on my pie. He is a talkative man in this place where we say so little. We all listened to his stories. Even Mother. Especially Mother.

He told of two patients lying ill in one room. One had brain fever, the other an aggravated case of mumps. They were so ill, Dr. McCabe said, that watches were needed at night, and he thought it doubtful either would recover.

Mother dabbed at her mouth with a napkin, listening. I had not seen her so attentive in months. She was absorbed in Dr. McCabe and his stories, forgetting her own discomfort.

Dr. McCabe told us he engaged a gentleman to watch these two patients through the night. The gentleman was to report any change in condition and wake the nurse periodically to administer medication. But the gentleman and the nurse both fell asleep. The man with the mumps lay staring at the clock and saw it was time to give the fever patient his medication. Unable to speak, or move any portion of his body except his arms, the mumps patient seized a pillow, and threw it as best he could, striking the watchman in the face.

Thus suddenly awakened, the watchman fell to the floor, startling both the nurse and the fever patient awake with the sound of his fall. Dr. McCabe grinned and, to my delight, Mother laughed aloud.

Dr. McCabe said the gentleman's fall to the floor struck the sick men as so ludicrous, they laughed heartily at it for some fifteen or twenty minutes. When Dr. McCabe came to see them in the morning, he found both of his patients improved . . . he said he'd never known so sudden a turn for the better. And now they are both well.

Mother joined us as we walked Dr. McCabe back to his skiff. She spoke to him in a way I had not heard her speak in some time. She spoke to Dr. McCabe as she would to a friend. Suddenly I was struck by how lonely Mother must be here.

Though Father was some distance away, inspecting the doctor's skiff for seaworthiness and preparing it for the short return back across the Ditch, I was close enough to hear Mother's words.

She asked Dr. McCabe to excuse the condition of the house. She told him she had not been well.

Dr. McCabe said he found nothing wanting but asked Mother to speak at greater length of her illness.

Mother said, "I detest the sea. It smashes and stinks and tears everything apart. It beats down my gardens and has left my health in ruins. My head aches, my joints ache, and every morning I wake swollen. My hands are useless."

To hear Mother speak this way pierced my heart.

Mother said Father should have taken a stag station, a station where the men live without their women, without their families. She said Father should never have brought us here. She told Dr. McCabe she was surely dying of damp and loneliness.

My heart reached out to Mother, but if Father had applied to a stag station as she said, I would never have seen him.

Oh, my diary, can't Mother see how much I need Father? Father understands the bigger world. He has brought the dawning of that understanding to me. There is a knowledge that reaches beyond the little cottage on Commerce Street, beyond Fenwick, even. Father's knowledge is more like the histories I read. To know the world only as Mother and Grandmother know it . . . perhaps that would be simpler. But my heart is filled with so many questions. And I am not certain I can find the answers in Mother and Grandmother's world.

Thursday, April 4, 1861
Rain. Wind E. Fresh.
Received and installed new glass to replace the cracked piece.

Fine fishing weather. Brought in a good catch of shad. The run of fish is so plentiful, there is enough for us to eat and shad left over to sell. Assistant lightkeepers do not command much of a salary. It is good to help out.

Thursday, April 11, 1861
Clear. Wind N.E. to E. Moderate.

There is much activity on the water to record.

Uncle Edward says a large number of troops — 3,000 men — have gathered in New York. Steamers and men-of-war stand in readiness.

The papers report that at Fort Sumter, in South Carolina, the supplies of the U.S. Government troops stationed there have been exhausted, and receiving fresh provisions will be a great risk. The Southern Confederacy might attack the Federal troops at any moment or at the very least force our Government to abandon the fort!

When I sleep, when I wake, when I watch over the Light, when I wind the clockwork or haul the barrels of oil, when I sit in the skiff, fishing, when I look across the great sea, when I watch over the children in the classroom, I feel in my heart a collision is about to take place somewhere.

I am beginning to think President Lincoln can't force the Southern states back into the Union any more than I can force Mother to be happy at the Light station.

That Jefferson Davis, so-called President of the Southern states — I like him less the more I hear of him. He knows President Lincoln can't abandon our men at Fort Sumter. President Lincoln won't leave our men there to die. It is a simple act of humanity. We have to bring supplies through to Fort Sumter.

Uncle Edward says telegraphic communication with the South has been cut off below Petersburgh, Virginia.

We may already be at war and not yet know. At war! With ourselves!

Saturday, April 13, 1861
Clear. Wind E.S.E. Moderate.

Keeper Dunne arranged to have the Light tower and the oil house whitewashed.

The painters arrived from the mainland early this morning. They rigged a barrel and tackle and swung out from the top of the tower to work. I did not believe when I saw who was part of the crew. Daniel Worthington. He nodded to me from the barrel.

When I finished my chores in the Light, I climbed down the spiral stairs to the observation deck. Daniel called to me and asked if I could bring him some water at lunch break. I was busy with housework through the morning, but I did not forget Daniel's request.

I brought him a big slice of pie in addition to the water he had asked for.

We sat on the beach with our backs to the dunes, and the Light, and my house.

"I still miss William," I said.

Daniel stared out to sea. "He never listened to anyone."

"He listened to me."

Daniel laughed. "And then he went and did exactly as he pleased."

I laughed, too. I knew he was right.

We talked about William and Mrs. Worthington and Daniel's little sisters. Daniel kept his eyes on the sea as he spoke. I noticed how long and thick his lashes are.

"I'm going to war as soon as President Lincoln calls," he said.

I told him perhaps there would not be a war.

Daniel turned his face from the sea a moment to look at me. His eyes were laughing. "Really, Amelia."

I could feel myself blush.

"Your mother might wish you to stay, you know," I said. "Your sisters need you."

"I can't stay," Daniel said.

His lips are full like William's were and his nose, like William's, straight and fine. And he has those pretty eyes, prettier than William's, I think. Big and gray with those long, thick lashes.

Daniel said he would work through the noon hour on Monday, and eat with me when I returned from school, if I liked.

I am eager for Monday.

Monday, April 15, 1861
Rain. Wind N.W. High.

The tide is the highest measured in nearly ten years.

Oda Lee has been out scavenging night and day. The sea leaves her gifts. Her cloak whips around her legs. She moves slowly, bending into the wind. Sometimes the sheer power of the wind lifts her off her feet, and she is a goodly weighted woman. She flaps like a crow from one piece of flotsam to the next.

The weather today was no good for painting Lighthouse towers. But Daniel came anyway. Just to see me. Because he'd promised. We ate our meal on the beach in our rain cloaks, watching Oda Lee.

Thursday, April 18, 1861
Clear. Wind N. to E. Fresh.

The weather for the past few days has been rainy, making painting impossible. With all his free time, Daniel rowed out every morning while I was doing my Lighthouse chores. Tuesday morning he said it was good to get out of a house filled with women, and his eyes laughed as he said so. It gave me an oddly pleasant feeling, knowing he sought refuge from the mainland in my company.

Yesterday morning, as Daniel rowed me across the Ditch from Fenwick to Bayville, we talked about slavery. "This fight over owning slaves has been too long in coming," he said. "Slavery is wrong, it always has been wrong, always will be wrong, no matter what color a person's skin." Daniel likes talking history as much as Uncle Edward, as much as I.

And I am always eager to hear what he thinks. I told him about the *History of the United States* I am reading and he listened with great interest and asked questions I had not thought of.

Monday, Tuesday, and yesterday, after school, we went together to visit Uncle Edward and Daisy. Daniel treats Daisy as if she never was a slave. I so enjoyed myself, I delayed returning home each day until the last moment, but Daniel had promised I would get back to Fenwick in plenty of time for the Light.

I would not mind if the weather kept the painting crew home all spring. It has made for very fine conditions for me to get to know Daniel better.

Today, though, it was lovely and clear, and Daniel worked while I rowed myself to and from Bayville.

Friday, April 19, 1861
Cloudy and Rain. Wind S. W. Fresh.

The War is begun!

Uncle Edward said Fort Sumter was attacked by General Beauregard of the Southern Confederacy on Friday last and though the Federal troops resisted, Major Anderson, the commander at the fort, had no choice but to surrender. Fort

Sumter has fallen to the secessionist rebels and the Stars and Stripes have been replaced by the "Stars and Bars" of the Southern Confederacy.

When I heard the news I felt a roaring inside my ears, a roar of outrage. That our country should come to this moment.

Sunday, April 21, 1861
Cloudy and Rain. Wind N.W. to N. High.

Keeper Dunne led us in prayer.

Uncle Edward said President Lincoln made a proclamation calling for 75,000 militia. He urges those in defiance of the law, all Secessionists, to return to their homes, and retire from this disagreement peaceably, and within twenty days.

President Davis says he is ready for President Lincoln's 75,000 Northerners.

Where is Delaware to stand? Kentucky refuses to send troops to fight for the Union. Yet in Rhode Island, the very Governor has offered his own services to President Lincoln. Men from all across the North prepare to put away their daily lives and march to war to uphold our Union.

Daniel is among them. But he is not without concerns. He worries about the welfare of his mother and sisters, as well he might. "Who will support them when I am away? Who will see to their needs?"

I did not know how to answer. But I could see the matter was of great concern to him, though it was not so great as to keep him from joining the Federal army.

Uncle Edward cannot go, because of his bad hand. But what of Father? Will Father join?

Monday, April 22, 1861
Cloudy to Rain. Wind N.E. High.

The schooner *W.B. Potter* foundered on the shoals north of Fenwick Station. Father and I brought all hands ashore safely and they stayed at the Fenwick quarters overnight.

The schooner went aground on Keeper Dunne's shift. He rang the alarm and woke Father and Father woke me and Mother. Father and I pulled on our storm clothes and fought the waves to push our boat off the island. We struggled to reach the distressed vessel. There were six aboard. All were glad to be rescued, but for the owner. The owner did not wish to leave his ship. What a foolish man. As if any possession could be more important than life itself. He screamed at Father, demanding a guard for the foundering ship. Father could hardly hear his words as the wind screamed in our ears, and the hungry waves swelled around us. The owner's mates, yelling into the storm, made the schooner's owner see the folly of his request. The schooner was already breaking up, being lifted and torn to shreds on the shoals. We were in danger of suffering the same fate, the storm was so wild, the waves and wind so high.

We got the crew and passengers safely back to Fenwick, though we had as difficult a time landing as we had pushing off. It took several attempts to bring the boat safely to shore.

Keeper Dunne remained at his watch at the Light, and Father and I led the men up the beach to the house and gave them blankets.

To my surprise and great relief I discovered that Mother, in our absence, had prepared food and warm drinks. My own body was so tired and so cold from the relief effort, I don't know how I could have done by myself all Mother did for us.

I can't remember when I've seen her so active, nor so beautiful. Do we need a wreck to make Mother happy?

Saturday, April 27, 1861
Clear. Wind S. Moderate.

I persuaded Mother and Father to attend Van Amburgh's Menagerie and Fair with me today. We stopped to inquire if

Grandmother might like to come with us. She declined. We next asked Uncle Edward, but he could not get away. He said we might see Daisy there, though. He had given her the day off.

The day was mild. By two o'clock, it seemed as if thousands were assembled on the grounds, all shades, colors, complexions, degrees, and kinds. I did not see Daisy, nor did I see Daniel, but there were so many people in attendance, they might have been there and I could easily have missed them.

I attended an exhibit in the Agricultural Booth. The exhibit featured the latest in farming equipment, tools that will replace the old reliable implements farmers have used for centuries. As I left, searching for Mother and Father, I wondered if in the future, lighthouses and their keepers would be replaced, too, just like farm tools. It does not seem possible. But I couldn't help fretting that someday there will be no Light, and no need for a keeper to tend it. That, and not seeing Daniel, turned my mood toward a dark and irritable humor.

Not only that, but if I had hoped to bring Mother and Father closer by this diversion, I was gravely mistaken. They quarreled all day — about the crowds, and what to eat, and where to go, and how long to stay there. And all their bickering, I realized, was not about the fair at all, but about something else, something unsaid. I did not see any point in remaining, but Father stubbornly insisted we stay.

When we finally returned home this afternoon, Mother's eyes were red and her hands swollen.

Before my watch, I walked carefully through the grasses where the plovers nest. I sat on the beach, thinking, as the long Atlantic rollers came in.

A little ways down the shore, Oda Lee stood in men's light trousers, her hands on her hips, talking to herself.

Tuesday, April 30, 1861
Fair. Wind S. Moderate.

Much depends upon Maryland. She grows more and more agitated, fearing a battle will soon be fought on her soil. Some of our neighbors, like Daniel, are joining the Union army, but many are not. At least our fellow Delawareans resist enlistment in the Confederate army. But if words were weapons, the North would surely suffer defeat in Sussex County.

The reports I hear in town are that the Confederate armies are in Virginia, preparing to make an attack upon Washington, our very capital.

In the newspaper, it states that Southern children of ten and twelve years of age have joined the regiments! Southern women, who never before turned their hand to anything because they had slaves to do their chores, now work day and night in the preparation of their men's equipage.

I work day and night, too. Not in preparation for battle. Just to keep the Light.

Wednesday, May 1, 1861
Fair. Wind S.W. Moderate.

The month of flowers, instead of bursting in all gay and sunlit, came in cold and blustery, more like February than May. The wind whipped up sand into a pelting storm. I checked the cover on the cistern to make certain sand would not foul our drinking water. The day was so disagreeable we were forced to light fires and wear hip boots, oil pants, overalls, layers of shirts, heavy sweaters, and overcloaks.

Uncle Edward said that in northern Delaware it was recommended that citizens raise money for the families of those who volunteer to defend the Government. "How else shall their families survive?" he said. "Men can't rise up and leave their homes without some support to make up for their absence." Daniel was greatly cheered by this proposal.

I am not surprised the idea originated in the north of the state. I wonder how our neighbors down here will take to it.

Mrs. Worthington is dependent on Daniel. He works not only as a painter. He will take any odd job to bring in money for his mother. I think about Father. What will we do if Father enlists? Will the Lighthouse Board pay me Father's salary? I doubt it. Mother and I would be destitute. And so would Grandmother, for Father supports her as well.

Uncle Edward said that Virginia has chosen to secede after all. The men of western Virginia are so unhappy with the situation, they have proposed separating their part of the state from the east so they might remain faithful to the Union.

So much anger, so much resentment. If only the two sides would sit down and discuss this sensibly. But how?

Mother cannot be sensible, nor can Grandmother. And Father, he is like a man deprived of his reason when the topic of slavery comes up. "There should be no slavery," he yells at Mother. "Not in the existing states, not in the territories."

Grandmother and I do not discuss politics. When I visited her today, she could speak of nothing but the mad dog that appeared in the street on Monday. A crowd of men went after the mongrel, but it managed to bite several dogs before it was killed. Unfortunately, those bitten also had to be destroyed. I think the mad dog is like South Carolina. It is biting its neighbors and forcing them into the position where they, too, must lose their lives.

Reenie O'Connell no longer comes to school. I wonder if she will continue to study on her own. And to draw. Her picture of the cottage is rain-damaged, but it is not ruined. I made a frame for Mother myself. The frame is not perfect. It irritates Father to look at it. Mother has it hanging in the front room.

Thursday, May 2, 1861
P. Cloudy. Wind N.W. Fresh.

Finished *A Chronological History of the United States.* Uncle Edward let me take his Darwin home with me.

The weather continues exceedingly cold for the season. Snow and hail and heavy frosts.

Governor Burton has proclaimed to the people of Delaware that the 780 men requested by the Secretary of War shall be assembled, though he does not command these men to obey President Lincoln. Rather, he suggests the men voluntarily offer their services in defense of the capital and the Constitution.

A request for arms has been sent to Europe. It seems we have more soldiers than weapons. Daniel said that will not stop him. He will take his father's musket down from the wall where it has hung all these years. Daniel will use his father's musket until the Government can issue him a weapon from its armory.

Daniel was one of the first to sign up. I am proud he is willing to fight for the Union. But I am so very frightened for his safety. I rely greatly upon his friendship and counsel. I shall miss him too dearly if he should truly leave.

I untied the bow from my hair and gave him the ribbon to carry with him, the green one Father gave me for Christmas, the one the color of the restless sea. Daniel laced the ribbon through his buttonhole and tied it in a knot. "I will keep it always, Amelia," he said.

I lowered my head. I did not wish him to see the pleasure on my face.

Friday, May 3, 1861
Clear. Wind N.W. High.

Today is my sixteenth birthday.

Mother's joints were so swollen, she could not get out of bed. I tended her, the house chores, and the Lighthouse chores. I rowed alone to school. . . . Daniel did not come out to meet me. I taught school, looked in on Grandmother and Uncle Edward. Picked up the mail. Then rowed myself back home. It was a day like every other day. Like every other day.

Uncle Edward was busy with inventory. He and Daisy worked together, counting the hoes and the shovels, the boots and the hats. They were discussing the War. What else? It is all anyone speaks of these days.

Daisy told me the slaves of Maryland are fleeing by whole families and in great numbers into Pennsylvania. Uncle Edward thinks this is just the beginning. He says not less than 500 slaves have escaped the South in the past few days.

Tonight, the thought of that tide of Negroes haunts me.

As I was writing this, standing watch at the Light, I heard a step on the stair below and I remembered when I heard steps but no one came. My whole body listened. I feared a ghost might appear at any moment. Whose ghost? Who is haunting me? And then I recognized the sound of the footstep.

It was Daniel. He came with a gift, a shell, delicate, polished, with a ribbon strung through it. He tied it around my neck. He wished me a happy birthday and left.

It happened so quickly, I'm still not certain I didn't imagine the whole thing. But here is the shell and the velvet ribbon.

Monday, May 6, 1861
Clear. Wind S.E. Moderate.

Both frost and ice this morning.

Wednesday, May 8, 1861
Rain to Fair. Wind N.E. Fresh.

A violent rain fell, quite deluging the lowlands, impeding the work of the farmers and bringing the sea to our doorstep.

Thursday, May 9, 1861
P. Cloudy. Wind N.W. to S.E. Moderate.

Volunteers are being interviewed in the state of Delaware.
　　When I asked Daniel what the interview was like, he said,
　　They ask:
　　Are you a married man?
　　Daniel's answer was no.
　　Have you anybody that cares anything about you?
　　No.
　　Oh, Daniel.
　　Do you believe in God?
　　No.

Daniel?
Do you believe in the Devil?
No.
Daniel!
Are you afraid to die?
No.
Have you ever been in the penitentiary?
No.
Have you ever stuck a knife in a man?
No.
Will you swear to bring home a lock of Jeff Davis's hair?
Yes.
You will do.

I asked Daniel is that truly the way the interview went? He smiled. I am not entirely certain but I believe he was teasing me.

Uncle Edward is going away for a week. He is traveling north, to Wilmington, to attend an abolitionist rally.

Before he left, he gave me the most wonderful new book, a belated birthday gift. It is a geography and atlas, published by Messrs. J. B. Lippincott & Co. Full-page maps of countries, states, and cities, maps of rain and winds and races of men . . . altogether the most satisfying book I have ever seen. Have set aside the Darwin for the moment. Before my watch I took the atlas out on the beach and, bundled up against the uncommon chill, sat reading as I faced out to sea.

The atlas does not fit inside my cloak as nicely as you, my diary. It is far too big. I cannot carry it up with me on watch. Anyway, I might become too engrossed and forget my duties.

North Carolina, Tennessee, and Arkansas have turned toward the Confederacy.

Maryland, it is settled, will stay with the Union. I am so relieved. If Maryland fell, Delaware could not have remained steady. We are just a stone's throw from the Maryland border. If Delaware fell, we would have lost the Lighthouse. It would have gone to the Confederates. And where would that have left us?

As far as I can figure, this War is not so much about the destruction of slavery as it is about the preservation of the Union. Yet if slavery should vanish from this country as a result of the Union's victory, I will not grieve.

I have spent my entire life in Bayville with Mother and Grandmother. I was wrong in my beliefs about slavery. Mother still is wrong, and Grandmother. But even if I did not think slavery wrong, it is pure selfishness to tear asunder what our forefathers struggled so hard to establish. Pure selfishness!

Monday, May 13, 1861
Cloudy. Wind N. Moderate.

It is rumored in town that women and their children are fleeing their Southern homes to avoid the danger of slave insurrections. The planters are loathe to leave their land unprotected from rebellious slaves. They refuse to let any of their white hands enlist in the Confederate army. They are arming them and keeping them as private guards, instead. The news is also that the Cotton States, particularly Mississippi and part of Louisiana, are running short of necessaries. Cornmeal, in small quantities, is the only food to be had.

I miss Uncle Edward. I should like to talk this over with him. I am eager for his return from Wilmington. Perhaps they are discussing the difficulties of the South at the abolitionist rally even now.

We should not be jubilant over the suffering of our Southern neighbors. It is a cruel thing to go hungry, no matter what your political beliefs. What does the stomach know of politics? It knows only that it is empty.

Tuesday, May 14, 1861
Clear. Wind N.E. Fresh.

In the paper appeared this Counsel to our Volunteers.

> *1. Remember that in a campaign more men die from sickness than by the bullet.*
>
> *2. Line your blanket with one thickness of brown drilling. This adds but four ounces in weight and doubles the warmth.*
>
> *3. Buy a small India rubber blanket (only 50 cents) to lay on the ground or to throw over your shoulders when on guard during a rainstorm. Most of the troops are provided with these. Straw to lie upon is not always to be had.*
>
> *4. The best military hat in use is the light-colored soft felt, the crown being sufficiently high to allow space for air over the brain. You can fasten it up as a Continental in fair weather, or turn it down when it is wet or very sunny.*
>
> *5. Let your beard grow, so as to protect the throat and lungs.*
>
> *6. Keep your entire person clean; this prevents fevers and bowel complaints in warm climates. Wash your body each day if possible. Avoid strong coffee and oily meat.*
>
> *7. A sudden check of perspiration by chilly or night air often causes fever and death — When thus exposed do not forget your blanket.*

I presented a copy of these instructions to Daniel, at his house, along with a pair of socks I've been knitting in the evenings, a blanket lined with drilling, and a small India rubber blanket I purchased with money I have made selling the fish I catch.

Daniel examined my package, bowed, and thanked me like a proper soldier.

Mrs. Worthington was not so formal. She hugged me and thanked me many times over.

I felt confused by Daniel's polite distance, but then he ran after me as I headed to the skiff. He caught me, swung me around, and taking my shoulders in his two large hands, gave me a kiss right on my forehead. Then, without a word, he ran back home.

Even now, as I stand watch, my cheeks flush with pleasure.

Thursday, May 16, 1861
P. Cloudy. Wind S.W. Moderate.

Pulled up five blue crabs from one pot and three from another this afternoon. Mother, though she is out of bed, is still painfully swollen and not able to get her fingers to work. After I steamed the crabs, I picked the meat. Mother smiled to see all the crabmeat. Her smiles come so infrequently, I felt as if a ray of sunlight had fallen across me.

Uncle Edward was delighted with the crabs I brought him. The rest sold marvelously well in town.

It is good to have Uncle Edward back from Wilmington and his abolitionist rally.

He said most of Delaware hates the Abolitionists.

I am disappointed to my very soul.

Uncle Edward said one side recognizes the rights of all men. The other side is based upon the domination of one race over another.

When put that way, how can so many stand against abolition? Yet a year ago, I stood against abolition.

I hardly see Daniel at all now. He does not come out to the island in the mornings. He is caught up in preparations for war.

Monday, May 20, 1861
Clear. Wind N. to E. Moderate.

Mother spends hours with the papers I bring her from Uncle Edward. She sits in silence, her hands so cramped she can barely turn the pages. Her chores are neglected. I would like to sit with the paper as she does. I would like to rest for an hour after school. Instead I run from one chore to the next. The only time I have to myself is on watch. And even this time isn't truly my own, for I must be always vigilant.

I don't know what is wrong with me. I feel angry much of the time. Peace is too often a stranger, except when I am here in the Light, or rowing across the Ditch, or with the children at school. But even the schoolchildren are stirred up by the War. Mr. Warner is enlisting in a few days, when school ends. He says he will be back in time for the commencement of fall classes. But what if the War doesn't end this summer? What if the War ends and Mr. Warner doesn't return?

My mind goes like this, in circles, angry at the North because they stubbornly corner the South, angry at the South because they pigheadedly challenge the North. Angry at my father because he has given up everything for his lofty principles. Angry at my mother because she cannot love him in spite of those principles.

This afternoon I lashed out at Mother when she ordered me to wash her underthings. And then I looked at her face, saw the pain in her eyes. And I knew suddenly what it cost her to ask me to do such a chore for her. Then I grew angry at myself.

Grandmother isn't well, either. I gave her rum to ease her aches. Rum is what she prefers. I did her heavy and light cleaning and asked Dr. McCabe to look in on her.

Seeing my stormy mood this afternoon, Uncle Edward searched for the words to cheer me. He told me not to brood about the War.

But how can I not brood?

Daniel came to see me last night to say good-bye. This time, when I heard the footstep on the stair, I knew it would be Daniel's face coming through the watch room door. And then he was there, his eyes shining, his fine frame proud and straight. He held me only a moment. "Good-bye, Amelia," he whispered in my ear. "Wait for me."

Then he was gone.

Thursday, May 23, 1861
Fair. Wind E. Moderate.

The fishing is the best I can remember. Rowed my catch to shore this morning and sold it in Bayville. Uncle Edward got first choice. Brought the rest to sell at the hotel. The additional money eases Mother's fretting. Mother always loved to look fashionable. She has not picked out new cloth for over six months, except perhaps for the aprons she made me at

Christmas. She is unable to sew now anyway because of the swelling in her fingers.

School ends tomorrow. Mr. Warner urged me to keep up with my reading and made a gift to me of several history books from his own collection. I shall miss Mr. Warner. I hope he fares well.

Uncle Edward said that oat and wheat crops have recovered exceedingly well from the unseasonable cold earlier this month. The yield promises to be heavy. Perhaps this will help keep the Union army fed.

The Delaware Regiment is assembling. Daniel is on the march.

Thursday, May 30, 1861
Clear. Wind S.E. Moderate.

Daniel's regiment is encamped one mile from Wilmington. I hope he is getting enough to eat. I hope his feet don't hurt. I hope that he is able to stay dry and sleep well.

The Stars and Stripes fly over Uncle Edward's store, though I see the flag nowhere else in town except at the post office and at school.

Traded my fish today for strawberries, which are large and ripe and sweeter than wild honey. Wish I could share them with Daniel. Instead I brought them back home and made shortcake for Father and Keeper Dunne.

Mother has lost interest in sweets. She has lost interest in most everything.

I fear this will not be a fast war. The Government is looking for more men. Men to fight for three years rather than three months. Father mumbles to himself. I overheard him this morning as he rubbed lamp rouge into the reflectors. Will he try enlisting?

If Father enlists in the Union army, that will push Mother away from him forever.

Thursday, June 6, 1861
Cloudy. Wind N.E. Fresh.

Uncle Edward has had word from his friend Warren Harris, who shipped out last August for Buenos Ayres on *The Pride of the Ocean*. Mr. Harris's ship had been at sea since before Mr. Lincoln's election and the unhappy events that have followed. Her crew had no knowledge that we had become, in their absence, a country at war with itself.

Warren Harris wrote Uncle Edward that when *The Pride of the Ocean* pulled into Apalachicola, in Florida, she was boarded by privateers under letters of marque issued by

Jefferson Davis. The captain and crew, including Mr. Harris, were taken prisoner and kept for over a week in a room without furniture or bedding, and fed only rice and water. With the help of the National Government, the captain and crew were at last able to regain their ship, but the privateers had stripped it of everything movable, including all clothing and food, except for a supply of rice for the trip back home to Boston. Those privateers are as thorough as Oda Lee. Uncle Edward said Mr. Harris's captain was lucky to get away with his ship. I think Uncle Edward is right.

As I write this on my watch, I look out toward the sea. Day and night, there are increased sightings of ships moving from North to South. Our log is filled with sightings and we must be ever watchful for signs of trouble. To see so much movement on the water excites me, but it also fills me with fear. Those ships are carrying boys as beloved to someone as Daniel is to me.

I purchased a copy of *The Soldier's Companion* in Bayville today for 25 cents and sent it to Daniel so he might know I am thinking of him.

Sunday, June 9, 1861
Rain. Wind S. Fresh.

Keeper Dunne led us in prayer.

Caught a feast of crabs. It felt good, out on the water, the rain falling softly.

Now I stand watch.

This war between neighbors means nothing to the sea. It is a very good lesson.

Thursday, June 13, 1861
Cloudy and Fog. Wind S.W. Light.

The shoals are shrouded in fog and we have kept the Light burning all day.

So far, no wrecks. Oda Lee sits like a cormorant out on the rocks, waiting for trouble. I cannot see her now. But I believe she is there still.

Mrs. Worthington had word from Daniel yesterday. His company left its encampment last Sunday, along with the other five companies in the Delaware Regiment.

Daniel will go to Maryland now. Three months is not so long.

I visit Mrs. Worthington every day. Today I helped her

pack a box of letter paper, envelopes, stamps, soap, and towels for Daniel. Being with his family, in his rooms, brings Daniel into my heart so that I can imagine him right beside me; I can almost smell him sometimes. Perhaps I miss him a little more when I am there. But I am still happy to be there, to be useful in Daniel's home.

Uncle Edward had news of a battle near Norfolk, Virginia. Two Federal regiments fired upon each other by mistake, killing two boys. Then the Federal troops united, only to be attacked by a rebel battery. Is it possible that thirty to forty Federal boys lost their lives, and nearly one hundred more were wounded?

The Government says the troops in the field, the three-month volunteers, shall be paid for their duty. This will ease Daniel's mind, and Mrs. Worthington's. Now, in addition to the pay for duty, the Government offers a $100 bounty if the three-monthers will enlist for three years before they are mustered out of service. Daniel's mother could live well on $100. But I wish Daniel would not sign on for so long. What if the War actually lasts three years?

When I stopped for the mail, there was a letter for me, from Daniel! I made myself wait until I could be alone here, in the Light, to read it.

Daniel's letter is most polite. But in one paragraph I see a flash of the Daniel I have come to know so well. This paragraph I shall copy out.

> *The health of the camp is good. The men are merry and happy as men can be. We have just enough work to make us relish sport. Target-firing, fishing, bathing, quoits, newspapers, &c fill up the time between drills and guard duty. At night all the noises of the barnyard can be heard from the quarters of Company D. Such crowing, Amelia, and cackling, and grunting, and bellowing were never surpassed by any living animals. The Kent boys are gaining a reputation of being great cooks. We have our batch of hot bread daily. It is not as good as your pie, nor my mother's duck, but it is mighty good anyway.*

Thursday, June 20, 1861
P. Cloudy. Wind S.W. Moderate.

Mother is not interested in the garden this year. Where last year she supervised me in the planting and weeding, this year I alone tend the roses, the turnips, the tomatoes and cucumbers.

I do not mind the extra work, particularly now that school

is out. It does not take much to tend this sandy garden. I am able to keep it weeded and watered. I love working in the garden. It holds me out of doors for hours with the wind and the smell of the sea and the sound of the breakers singing in my ears.

Why can it not be the same for Mother? Why can't the sea bring her the peace it brings me?

Friday, June 21, 1861
Clear. Wind S. W. Light.

Dr. McCabe's brother came into Uncle Edward's store while I was there today. He has known almost a week now about his son, who was killed in Maryland while on guard at the railroad bridge over the Big Elk. Dr. McCabe's nephew was killed by an oncoming train. His body will be returning to Delaware any day now. The McCabe family had hoped he would be home soon. But not like this.

Saturday, June 22, 1861
Rain and Fog. Wind S.E. Light.

We are having a fine fall of rain. The heavy clouds and sheeting downpour kept Father, Keeper Dunne, and me busy all day and now into the night on fog shift at the Light. The log is filled with entries recording wind, conditions, behavior of the lamps, &c. The bell-buoy boat, repaired and freshly painted, clangs out its warning. Mother has kept to her bed with the curtains drawn and the windows shut.

Tuesday, June 25, 1861
Rain and Fog. Wind S.E. Light.

I cannot explain how I knew a ship had gone aground on the sandbar last night during my watch. I could not see it. And yet I felt it like a scraping inside me.

I'd been watching the lights of passing ships the best I could, but the fog made tracking nearly impossible. The crew of the yacht did not hear the bell-buoy boat ringing its warning.

I hesitated to wake Father and Keeper Dunne. I had no proof that anything was amiss. Just a "feeling." I hesitated, also, to bother Mother unnecessarily.

Standing out on the balcony, the rain slashing against my face, I thrust my head toward the sea and listened. It was then I heard the shouts of men and a faint sound, a ghostly sound, like a woman crying from the depths of the sea.

This time I did not hesitate. I rang the alarm bell and within minutes Father and Keeper Dunne joined me.

When their hearts and their breathing stilled enough, they heard, too, the cry of terror from a woman, the calls for help from deep-voiced men.

Keeper Dunne and Father rowed out toward the sound. Fortunately the waves were not high and they did not have to fight anything more than the fog and the rain. But I could hear the cries of panic increase as the pleasure yacht slowly gave way and slipped under the water.

Father and Keeper Dunne brought back the four crew members and all five of the passengers, including the woman I had heard. She wept softly as Father helped her up the beach to the house. I could see the lamp burning upstairs in the kitchen window. Mother could be counted on even in her sad condition. She cared for our unexpected guests through the night until this noon, when they were all questioned by the insurance company and returned to the mainland.

Last night, after all the members of the sailing party, their crew, Father, and Keeper Dunne had disappeared inside the house, a deadly quiet settled back over the Light. The sea hardly moved. Nothing moved.

Until I saw the lantern. Oda Lee, floating through the fog, seeing if there was anything left to scavenge.

Thursday, June 27, 1861
P. Cloudy. Wind S.E. Moderate.

Uncle Edward said today that several of the area farmers are arranging to take a day off for observation of the Fourth. This is not an easy time for them to be away from their fields. Both the hay and wheat are heavy and ready for the scythe. Yet for these men it is important to show their loyalty. I am so glad to know of them.

Daisy has gone off to Pennsylvania for a week and Uncle Edward asked if Father and Mother and I might like to come across the Ditch this evening and share a meal with him. I rowed back excitedly and asked, but Keeper Dunne had other plans and could not let both of us go. I suggested that Mother and I could go without Father. Perhaps we could bring Grandmother to Uncle Edward's with us. Mother hesitated. I could see how much she longed to get off the island and see Grandmother. But she had kept to her bed most of the day because of the swelling in her joints. In the end she did not think she could bear the motion of the boat across the Ditch.

The only thing that keeps my spirits buoyed is this letter I received from Daniel.

Here I am in Maryland, a high private in the U.S. army, a place a few weeks ago I had no expectation of seeing. I had hoped to make it at least to Washington but rumor has it the Government isn't sure it can trust those of us from Delaware.

We are getting along very well on the feed we get. Hard crackers and salt pork are not the most palatable viands, but I remember, Amelia, how you told me of the sufferings of our Revolutionary sires, and I am careful not to complain. You and your great mind full of history, you take all the fun out of being miserable.

Our victuals are not set before us by servants, or by a sister or mother, I assure you. We wash our own dishes, and, for that matter, sometimes our own clothes. Ah well, I am happy, for I am here for my country's sake.

Our Sundays are not spent here as at home. That day is like all others to us. Plenty of drill and very little church.

The floors on which we lie are made of peculiarly hard wood — not a soft plank to be found. All the better, it will accustom me to hardships. But what a fall it is from a comfortable bedstead and mattress. Never mind. If I had to fall in this life, at least I did not fall from the barrel at the top of your Lighthouse.

The sights of Maryland are not so different from our own state, though there are places from history that might interest you. As for me, I wish I could be back in Bayville for a few hours. Here we are surrounded by men, no ladies' society whatsoever. It is hard to imagine I ever looked for an excuse to leave my sisters and mother in that gracious house of women. I am afraid, with respect to my present companions, I will become a regular bear and lose all my refinement — that is, if I ever had any.

I cannot help but smile, even as I copy this. Bless Daniel. To make me smile at such a time.

Thursday, July 4, 1861
Clear. Wind S.W. Fresh.

Last night, I kept an even more careful watch than usual as all through the night the crack of pistols and guns could be heard across the Ditch, announcing the arrival of our country's Independence Day. It was all in good fun, but my ear listened to every noise, lest it warn of danger and duty. The firing of guns may mask another sound that would tell of disaster on the shoals. Fortunately no such disaster occurred through the night. At sunrise the church bells rang.

Father and I cleaned and polished the big panels of bull's-eyes and prisms in the lantern room as quickly as possible so we could get a start on the day.

I asked Mother last evening if she would accompany us to the Fourth of July program in Lewes and she agreed. But when she woke this morning, she found it a particularly bad day. She urged us to go on without her. Keeper Dunne agreed to look in on her from time to time.

Mother's hand trembled when I came to say good-bye, but she said I must not be concerned. I must have a lovely day.

Uncle Edward had posted a notice that his shop would be closed. Daisy has not yet returned from Pennsylvania.

We arrived by wagon in Lewes just before ten, in time to watch the long procession of clergymen, orators, choirs, committees, cadets, citizens on foot, citizens on horseback, citizens in carriages, and a company of guards. Two large American flags draped the archway under which the orators spoke. Evergreens and flowers festooned the whole platform. The Reverend prayed for our country, for a happy issue out of its present difficulties, for a pardon of our individual and national sins, and a blessing upon the troops defending our liberties. The Declaration of Independence was read and more speakers addressed the crowd.

Late afternoon, Father and I left Uncle Edward off in Bayville, returning to the island in time to light the lantern. I regretted we could not stay in Lewes for the fireworks, but as I walked out on the narrow gallery, I saw the displays of brilliant lights at sea and on land.

Sunday, July 7, 1861
Fair. Wind S.E. Moderate.

President Lincoln is calling for 400,000 more men.

Tuesday, July 9, 1861
P. Cloudy. Wind S.E. Light.

General Scott says, "Make haste slowly."
It is advice that works equally well at a lighthouse.

Thursday, July 11, 1861
Clear to Rain. Wind S.E. to N.W. Moderate.

Grandmother wanted to gossip when I came to do her chores. She said that Ann Blackiston has left her husband, and he has posted notices everywhere that he will not be responsible for any charges she contracts. I beat the rugs ruthlessly from the porch and weeded Grandmother's flower beds in the rain. But I could not escape the fact that wives leave husbands, husbands leave wives. If a country can break its bonds, why not two people?

But Mother and Father must reconcile. When a storm comes, everyone is needed to run the Lighthouse station. Father, Mother, and I work together alongside Keeper Dunne, each with our own tasks, to meet the storm head on, and to survive it. And might not another country act like a storm? What if England, or France, or Spain decides we are weak now? It would be easy for them to come blustering in and conquer us.

I feel as if I am the Light in my family. I must keep my hope burning, so that Father and Mother, even in the darkness that seems to engulf them, might find their way back.

Monday, July 15, 1861
Clear. Wind S.E. Fresh.

A comet appeared recently in remarkable brilliancy, although now it is fading. It is called Thatcher's comet, after the man who discovered it last April. But everyone calls it the "war comet." Every night, after my watch, I go out and sit on the beach and send up my troubles to it.

The weather has been very warm for several days, the mercury rising to the suffering altitude of 96 degrees in the shade. As hot as it is, the chill never leaves the room where Mother and Father are present.

Thursday, July 18, 1861
Clear. Wind N. Fresh.

I thought it would be Father leaving, to fight for the Union, but it is Lightkeeper Dunne who has left us. He said nothing to us of his intentions until this very day. He simply waited for the arrival of the new Keeper and departed. I never did grow fond of Keeper Dunne, though he was a good enough Lightkeeper. Still I don't know anything about the new Keeper. Father and I will be busy until Keeper Hale is accustomed to this station. I am most relieved that Father is staying, at least for the moment.

Mother hoped that Father would be promoted from Assistant Lightkeeper to Head Keeper, but the Lighthouse Board will never consider such action because of the mark on Father's record.

I am not certain how I shall stand with Keeper Hale. He has a handful of rosy children, and he and his wife are as big and boisterous as whales. They treat me as a child. Keeper Hale laughs when I tell him I am an equal in the keeping of the Light. I cannot suffer the thought of losing my place here. I shall never relax around him. Fortunately his children are not old enough to help with the Lighthouse duties, and they will keep his wife so busy she will be no help, either. Soon enough, Keeper Hale will see the value of my extra hands, my extra ears, my extra eyes.

Oda Lee cut through the piney woods in front of me while I was gathering kindling for the house.

She stopped and stared at me. She had never held still so close to me before. I didn't know what to do. Finally, to break the silence, I told her Keeper Dunne had left.

Oda Lee was quiet awhile. "I know," she said. "They all go in the end."

Sunday, July 21, 1861
Clear. Wind S.E. Light

A flock of black skimmers rested out on the shoals, making a great noise this morning as Keeper Hale led the lot of us in prayer.

I played with Keeper Hale's children this afternoon. I was not certain we should be so noisy on the Sabbath. But Keeper Hale did not discourage us. There are five little Hales, three girls, two boys, none older than eight. The oldest girls, Sarah and Alice, have a gift for fancy. They make up games all day to keep the three smallest ones, Mary, James, and William, entertained. They cheer me. They are so full of laughter and life. Even their rooms, so dark when Keeper Dunne occupied them, are dappled now with sea light. Mrs. Hale asked if there were not any berries on this whole island, and Keeper Hale came along as we went on a hunt for them.

Keeper Hale acted like a great bear as we marched through the woods, and the children ran screaming back to me every time he growled. They peeked around my legs, drawing my skirts about them. We ate plenty of berries during our outing. But we brought back enough to satisfy Mrs. Hale's recipe for berry pie.

Monday, July 22, 1861
Clear. Wind N. Moderate.

Keeper Hale, Father, and I talked as we polished the lenses and the reflectors this morning. With each passing day Keeper Hale permits me to do more of my normal Lighthouse chores.

There is an ease between Father and Keeper Hale. I believe they are friends already in a way Father and Keeper Dunne never were. I have never known Father to have a friend other than Uncle Edward. It is good for him to have someone here to speak with.

As we worked, Keeper Hale told us of his sister who lives in South Carolina. She grew up in the North and has no fondness for slavery. Nor does her husband. They have servants, but they are paid, much as Uncle Edward pays Daisy.

Father said, "Imagine living in South Carolina and supporting the Union, Wickie. If the rebels despise the Union at a distance, how much more they must despise their Union neighbors."

He asked if Keeper Hale's sister and her family were safe in South Carolina.

Keeper Hale opened his huge arms and said jovially that she could come here and stay with him if she wanted. I do not know where he would put one more person. His rooms are filled to the edges with children and books and the most fascinating possessions.

Later, when Father and I were alone working in the garden, we came close to each other as we moved down the rows, plucking out weeds. "It must be like that for Mother," I said. "The way it is for Keeper Hale's sister. Surrounded by people who feel different from you."

"It is hardly the same, Wickie," Father said. But he would say no more.

Tonight, as I stand watch, I have so much to think about. Keeper Hale's sister has made a life for herself in South Carolina. She loves her home there as I love mine here. We have been at Fenwick Light from the start. We were here when Keeper Dunne touched the lucerne to the very first wick for the very first time. I remember the tiny flames growing behind their prisms. I remember those flames within their glass lenses. . . . Those lenses reminded me of flower petals when I first saw them. I remember the lantern room becoming a cage of light.

We have kept the Light burning here ever since, so that no more lives would be lost in the dangerous waters off our stretch of the Delaware shore.

Mother says that Father has no understanding of his

responsibilities. When she speaks to him at all, it is to remind him of his past mistakes. To accuse him of present mistakes. She says if Father understood his responsibilities, he would never have stranded us on Fenwick Island.

I wonder about Mother's words, about Father's choices. Does responsibility to family weigh more than responsibility to something greater?

I have never seen Father do anything but honor his responsibilities at the Light. He would sooner die than let Fenwick Light become a Dark House, an extinguished lighthouse. A Dark House is deadly. The Lightkeeper must carry the consequences of that darkness for a lifetime.

But what of our own lives? Are we a Dark House, Mother, Father, and I? After watching Keeper Hale and his family, what else can I think? And if our life is a Dark House, whose responsibility is it? And what are the consequences? And how long must those consequences be carried?

Saturday, July 27, 1861
Clear. Wind N.W. Fresh.
Inspection at 10 A.M. Condition very good.

From Manassas Junction, Virginia, along Bull Run, there is word of a slaughter of Union soldiers. The Union troops were vastly outnumbered and exhausted. They panicked and rushed into retreat. The losses are frightful. Wagons are arriving in Alexandria and Washington, carrying dead and wounded.

I pray Daniel was nowhere near the action.

Thursday, August 1, 1861
Clear. Wind S.E. Light.

Keeper Hale has decided that on Sunday we shall raise a pole here at Fenwick Island from which to fly a large national flag. All citizens from on and off the island who are loyal to the Union are invited to attend the flag raising. Keeper Hale thundered up our stairs this morning to ask Mother to help Mrs. Hale provide refreshments. Generously, he gave her an allowance with which to do so. I do not know where he found the money to undertake such an affair.

After he bounded down the stairs again, Mother muttered, "I'll not labor with that abolitionist wife of his. Nor will I lift a finger to help the man who has taken your father's position."

Mother is weary beyond her limit, and present circumstances have not improved her temper. Keeper Hale's children are noisy, night and day. To me it is a joyful sound, but the precious little sleep Mother once got is lost to her with all the commotion of those busy children.

Keeper Hale does not know how to deal with Mother. He believes everyone enjoys the same good health and robust constitution he and his family enjoy.

I told Mother I would take the money and go to Bayville and get supplies for her. "I'll work with the Keeper's wife."

Mother shook her head. She would not part with Keeper Hale's money.

"Mother, you can't just take it."

"Why not? We have so little. Your father should be Head Keeper."

I do not have enough money to buy supplies for Keeper Hale's refreshments myself. The money I earn selling fish disappears as soon as I purchase more medicine for Mother from Dr. McCabe.

But Keeper Hale is expecting refreshments contributed by our family.

Rather than fighting with Mother, I decided I'd better catch some fish to sell, in the hopes of earning what Mother would not part with. I picked my way over the ribbons of rotting seaweed, dragging the skiff down to the water's edge. The gulls wheeled overhead.

Oda Lee appeared from nowhere just as I prepared to push off.

"Fine day," she said.

I jumped. Then tried to hide the fact that she had startled me. I brushed wisps of hair back from my face, speechless.

Oda Lee asked me if I had a crab in my knickers.

I laughed.

Then I told Oda Lee about the new Keeper and his party on Sunday.

Oda Lee asked if the new Keepers were Abolitionists.

I nodded.

She wanted to know how Mother felt about her new neighbors.

I looked down and said I didn't know.

This time it was Oda Lee's turn to laugh.

I always thought Oda Lee so peculiar. But today, she understood not only what I said to her, but what I did not say, as well.

Sunday, August 4, 1861
Cloudy. Wind S.E. Light.

Keeper Hale led us in prayer at dawn. Services with Keeper Hale are unlike any services I have ever attended in all my life.

Keeper Hale's words are full of glory and goodness and bounty and life. Not a dark or somber word escapes his mouth.

Saw Oda Lee out on the beach early this morning. While she scavenged, Father, Keeper Hale, and I carried oil up from the oil house and filled the reservoirs. We cleaned and brightened every pane of glass and every reflector, polished every piece to brilliancy, the brasswork, too. Then I drew the curtains and washed down the rooms. When I looked again, Oda Lee was simply sitting on the beach, her arms resting on her knees, staring out to sea. Napoleon sat beside her.

When I came out of the Lighthouse, Oda Lee motioned to me.

I looked back at the house to see if Mother might be watching, then came across the dunes, my hands stained and smelling of lamp rouge.

Oda Lee never looked at me once, the entire time I approached her. Instead she kept her eyes on the sea. I kept turning back toward the second-story window of our house. The window where Mother stands.

While I turned to look back the last time, Oda Lee slipped away. For a moment, I thought of the time in the Lighthouse when I was on watch and I heard a footstep on the stair, but then no one came to me in the watch room.

I walked through the dune grass to where Oda Lee had

been sitting and nearly tripped over a basket set right in the path. The basket was filled with supplies. I had managed to purchase a few things. But in the basket was all I needed to help with Keeper Hale's party. The basket came from Oda Lee. Who else?

But why did she leave it for me? I am much unnerved by her.

For a moment I hesitated, uncertain about whether I should take the basket or not. These supplies were from Oda Lee's scavenging expeditions.

But then Mrs. Hale called to me.

And without a second thought, I lifted the basket and ran all the way back to her.

Mrs. Hale and I set straight to work with the baking. The party was set for four in the afternoon.

We had help from the children, who were sticky up to their elbows and streaked with flour across their cheeks and foreheads. Even Keeper Hale was put to work after he and Father had set the pole.

At four, with everyone cleaned back up, we waited, looking across the Ditch. Uncle Edward came with Daisy, though he was reluctant to leave the store unattended. Still, he said it was important for both of them to come. While we waited for the others, Uncle Edward told us that someone sent a parcel to the editor of *The Smyrna Times*. It looked as if they were return-ing a copy of the paper from several days past, but when the bundle was unwrapped, a yard of brown domestic cloth with blood and scabs fell out. Smallpox! Someone had attempted to infect the editor and his staff at *The Smyrna Times* with small-pox. They are a pro-Union paper. Fortunately no harm was done.

No one else ever came to Keeper Hale's party.

Keeper Hale never lost his good spirits. Nor did Mrs. Hale. We made a picnic out of it and had a wonderful time.

Mother stayed in her room.

Oda Lee came out and stood a good distance down the beach. When we raised the national flag, she turned her back on us and walked away.

Thursday, August 8, 1861
Clear. Wind S.E. Light.

I saw what Keeper Hale wrote about me to the Lighthouse Board. He says I am a sturdy girl, frugal in all things, even lan-guage. He states that I carry equally one-third of the Keeper's responsibilities, and my logs and attendance to duties are be-yond reproach. He recommends not only that I be retained in the service of the Fenwick Light, but that I be compensated for my work. I was not certain I would like Keeper Hale or his noisy family when they first arrived. I was not certain he would permit me to remain at my Lighthouse duties. I judged him wrongly.

Grandmother has come out to the station to help with Mother as Mother's health has taken a turn for the worse. Grandmother complains about the children downstairs at every opportunity. Yet I am so fond of them.

The change the Hales have brought to this island is wonderful. Downstairs, in Keeper Hale's quarters, there is always a river of voices. There are thumps and bangs and shouts and laughter. It is a sweet sound. But Grandmother criticizes with every breath. I feel as if our rooms are suddenly too small.

I wake to the sound of the Hale children singing and chattering. Those happy sounds fill me with a contentment I have never known before. Today Sarah and Alice raced up the Lighthouse stairs as I was polishing the brass. They would not leave me alone until I promised to come swimming with them. Yesterday, I took little Mary out in the skiff and taught her to fish. The children are forever drawing me into their games. James and William spend hours and hours building forts in the sand, only to bash them down in a matter of seconds, gleefully, with their plump little feet. Mary and James take particular pleasure in chasing Napoleon around the house, across the dunes, along the beach, and I chase after them . . . to make certain no harm comes to either child or cat. Napoleon could escape from them in a moment if he was truly annoyed, but he likes their attention as much as I.

Father has given his cot to Grandmother and is sleeping here at the Light. That gives us more time together, though now I must steal time to write in you, my diary. In silence, this afternoon, Father and I watched the gulls and herons. From high above we studied the movements of the sandpipers and the sanderlings, the knots and the yellowlegs, the curlews and the oystercatchers. I tried to talk with Father about Mother. But Father stopped me. He said there are certain things that should not be discussed between father and child. I will try to respect and obey Father. But it is hard to live with so many questions.

The news is full of skirmishes in Missouri and Kansas, and in Maryland. The Delaware regiment is not involved. People in Bayville continue to speak of the devastation done to the Union troops at Bull Run last month. I am grateful for every day Daniel is not in battle.

Grandmother brought peaches with her when she came. I baked three peach pies. Mother's favorite is peach pie. But I could not get her to take even the smallest taste. Happily, Grandmother succeeded where I failed.

Keeper Hale and his family were delighted with the extra pie I made for them.

I do not know what Oda Lee thought of hers. I left it on the path in the basket placed precisely where I had found it filled with supplies a week ago.

Sunday, August 11, 1861
P. Cloudy. Wind E. Moderate.

Keeper Hale led us in prayers of celebration this morning.

This afternoon, Uncle Edward explained the Confiscation Bill to me, the one just passed in Congress. If property is discovered, especially property devoted to the uses of the Rebellion, that property may be confiscated and sold. When the property involved is a slave, the United States Government will not take the role of slave trader. The slave shall be set free.

I wish no one would come to the island for a while, and that I did not have to leave it. I wish that Father and the Hales and I could just keep the Light and not see anyone, not talk to anyone until this lunacy is over, until the country is the country again, and there is peace. I wish we could go back . . . back to before South Carolina seceded, back to before Mother and Father began their fights. But how far back would we have to go?

Beginning tomorrow, school resumes. How odd it will seem without Mr. Warner. The new head teacher is from Maryland. I do not know how we shall manage together.

Five companies of the Delaware Regiment returned to Wilmington Saturday, their three months having expired. The report is that they are in good health. They have been engaged in watching bridges in Maryland and have not seen even a skirmish. They will be paid off in a day or two, then mustered out of service.

Daniel has signed on with the Second Delaware Regiment for three years, but I believe he must be mustered out of the three-month regiment first. Mrs. Worthington had a letter from him on Friday. We don't know where he is now. I brought Mrs. Worthington some shad yesterday and visited with her a spell. Daniel's little sisters like to climb into my lap. They want stories about the barefooted Hale children. They want stories about Daniel. They miss their big brother. I miss their big brother, too.

I try to be civil with Grandmother. She has softened a little. Watching Mother in such pain has softened us all. Grandmother pats Mother down with a cool dampened cloth in the dark bedroom. Outside the curtains is the brilliant light of the sea, but in Mother's room it is as still and dark as a grave.

Rain has fallen every day since Grandmother arrived. Today

the decision was made to take Mother back to town with Grandmother. It is a decision we all knew would come, though Father put it off as long as possible, I think, for my sake.

Mother and Grandmother shall leave as soon as the weather clears. In the meantime, I have kept the fire stoked for Mother though it is August.

Abraham Lincoln has asked us to set aside the last Thursday in September as a day of prayer and fasting for all the people of the nation. It will be difficult to perform our duties and keep to the President's proclamation, but we shall try.

Thursday, August 15, 1861
Fair. Wind S.W. Fresh.

Mother left with Grandmother this afternoon. Father and I took them across the Ditch. I looked over my shoulder at the familiar lines of the Lighthouse, the white conical tower topped with its black balcony. Mother looked back at it, too.

Father lifted and carried Mother easily to Commerce Street. We settled her comfortably in Grandmother's bed.

After taking care of her at the Lighthouse through all these months of bad spells, I did not know how I could leave her today.

"Should I stay here with Mother?" I asked Father as we stood in Grandmother's front room.

Father shrugged.

If I stayed, it would be just like before, when Father was gone at sea, and the three of us lived in the cottage together. I looked at Grandmother, more active than she has been in a long time. She has revived with Mother's needing her. I realized it would be better for her to nurse Mother without me.

I chose to come back to the Light.

How odd it feels here on Fenwick without Mother.

Thursday, August 22, 1861
Clear. Wind N.E. Fresh.

Daniel is back! I am so filled with joy. He will be here for three weeks. Three weeks! I forced myself to do justice to my chores before Father and Keeper Hale told me I had done enough.

I rowed quickly to the mainland and stopped in at Grandmother's, but Mother was sleeping. Then I raced to the Worthingtons' in the moments I had before school. Daniel and I were awkward at first with each other.

But then we went out in the skiff after school, fishing. I dropped my line and sat quietly, waiting for Daniel to speak.

Knowing if I could be still long enough he would eventually talk.

And he did start talking. He said it is so different here in Delaware. The way people talk about the War, the way they talk against President Lincoln. "The War is easier to understand when you discuss it with like-minded people."

I asked him to explain it to me.

He told me the things I already knew. That the slave states wanted to expand slavery into the new territories, that their pride forced them to turn their backs on the Union when they could not have their way.

"Nothing can be accomplished by secession," Daniel said. "The South has nothing to gain. This could have been worked out without leaving the Union. If they felt their rights were being invaded, the Constitution was there to aid them."

I sat in the skiff, my line in the Ditch, the marsh and reed birds singing. And Daniel. It is a moment I shall always remember.

Daniel thought he might switch regiments. He said some of the officers are good men, but not all. "It helps to know the man who's leading you. I've been lucky so far. There was a colonel I knew who didn't care a fig about his men."

Daniel gazed across the water. He sighed deeply, more deeply than the first time we really talked after his brother,

William, died. "Our Government didn't plan this War as well as it might have." Daniel tilted his head, listening to the call of a reed bird. I could have watched him like that forever.

He said the rebel army is growing daily. But the three-monthers from the Federal army are being sent home. The capital is not adequately protected. Everywhere, there are too few Federal troops. They must bring the three-monthers back into position immediately. And the press must cease printing where the troops are, where they are heading, how many. "No wonder the rebels are taking the advantage."

We sat in the boat a long time, quiet. "When do you think it will end, Daniel?"

"Prepare for a long war, Amelia. Bull Run was lost because everyone up North thought the War would be short. We thought that victory would be easy. We were wrong. We need a vast army, we need ample supplies. That's the only way to win. The battle at Bull Run extended over seven miles. Seven miles of soldiers! Seven miles of death."

We brought the fish we caught back to Daniel's house. I shared an early meal with his family before heading home for my watch. When I shut my eyes, even now, I can see Daniel in the boat with the reed birds behind him.

Sunday, August 25, 1861
Clear. Wind S.E. Fresh.

Keeper Hale led us in a celebratory service before chores.

Daniel rowed over early to help with the brass. He gets on well with Keeper Hale. I almost felt left out. But then Daniel had to rush back to attend regular church with his mother and sisters. I am glad for Keeper Hale in a hundred different ways, not least of which is the way he keeps the Sabbath.

Father brought Mother back to the station today for a visit. I was overjoyed to see her here, in her own home. We spent the day together. She looks better. I have watched her steady progress each day during my visits to Grandmother's cottage.

How much better she is than when Father carried her out of here ten days ago.

She did not enjoy her time back on the island, though. Keeper Hale's children buzzed curiously around her and Mother swatted them away like they were bothersome insects.

Father came upon us while I was brushing Mother's hair in her old bedroom. She had made a new dress for me and I was wearing it. Father stood in the doorway a moment, watching us. His expression clearly showed what pleasure he took in seeing the two of us together like that. Then Mother caught sight of Father standing there and told him to leave at once. A wounded look crossed Father's face for only a moment. Then he straightened, bowed, and was gone.

I took Mother back myself to Grandmother's cottage and returned to Fenwick before sunset. I tried talking with Father about Mother when I returned. Father turned away.

Thursday, August 29, 1861
Fair. Wind S. Fresh.

School this morning. After checking on Mother this afternoon, I met Daniel and we hurried off to Uncle Edward. Uncle Edward visited with us for nearly an hour. He has a great deal of time on his hands these days. He says it would be so even if he was surrounded by Unionists. It seems the only businesses doing well in Delaware are those supplying the army — makers of shoes and coats and weapons.

He told us of a new business recently sprung up in the South — slave stealing. Uncle Edward says hundreds of men are descending on the eastern section of Virginia. There are plenty of slaves running loose there, slaves who have been deserted by their masters. These men take the abandoned slaves and convey them down to South Carolina, Georgia, and Alabama, where they are condemned to slavery forever.

I was hardly able to take in that news when he told us that

Jeff Davis has issued a proclamation ordering all Union sympathizers to depart within forty days. He means to seize their property, to fill his treasury.

What will happen to Keeper Hale's sister and her family?

I tried to ask Father about this earlier tonight. He is still sleeping below, rather than in the house. In spite of his nearness, there is a great distance between us. It grows greater by the day. I asked him to come and sit with me awhile on my watch. He came but he hardly listened, not when I spoke of Union sympathizers in the South, not when I spoke of Daniel. When I was little, and he was a stranger, someone I saw only briefly with months of absence between, he used to pull my braid in teasing when I was hesitant to speak to him. He would look straight into my eyes. "Go on, Amelia," he would say. As if everything on my mind was important to him.

There is no "Go on, Amelia," now. Only distance.

Thursday, September 5, 1861
P. Cloudy to Rain. Wind S.W. Moderate.

I am an official Assistant Lightkeeper with a salary, small but steady! I picked up the letter today at the post office. When I showed the letter to Father and Keeper Hale, they held a little ceremony for me. Then Father placed the letter in a box containing his most important papers.

I am considering giving up my duties at Bayville School in order to take on more here at the Light. It is hard for me to imagine not being in the classroom with my little scholars, but everything has changed since Mr. Warner's departure. Perhaps I could help teach the Hale children here on the island, instead.

I stopped in on Mother and Grandmother this afternoon and the Worthingtons, too, to show Daniel the letter from the Lighthouse Board, but signs of a storm made me head back to the Light early, without a visit to Uncle Edward.

Daniel has one week more. The time passes too quickly.

Daniel walked me back to the skiff in the rain this afternoon. He had heard from someone in his regiment that the English were seeking, among their possessions, a place where cotton might be grown. Once they have a source of cotton other than our Southern states, the English will not need to wait for our blockade on the Southern cotton export to lift.

But what happens to the Negro who knows no other work than picking in the cotton fields if the cotton supply is no longer needed? Look what has come of the rebel's temper.

In less than a month, all the people of Tennessee who adhere to the General Government shall lose their property.

Those same Union sympathizers, if they choose to remain in the state of Tennessee, shall find themselves jailed.

Father, Keeper Hale, and I cleaned and inspected all the gutters and joints in anticipation of a strong blow. The cistern in the cellar is low. A good rainfall will do wonders for our supply of fresh water.

The storm is gaining strength, lashing around me now, as I stand watch. The wind is gusting, buffeting the tower. Spears of lightning are cast quickly toward the lantern room, then are swallowed by the bright flashing beacon of light. Thunder rolls in, regular as the wild waves, one crack rumbling into the next. The sky is fitful, with long legs of lightning kicking out every few seconds. The bell clangs for all it is worth. I cannot hear the bell in a storm without thinking of Mother.

Thursday, September 12, 1861
Fair. Wind N.W. Fresh.

Father left before dawn this morning, while Keeper Hale was on last watch. Father did not speak with me about the purpose for his leaving. He has not talked much with me since Mother came to visit last month. I have been thinking a lot about that visit. Mother was cruel to Father, crueler, in fact, than she was to the Hale children.

It troubles my spirit, these changes. The longer Mother is away from the Light, the happier and stronger she appears. But Father is not at peace. Even with Keeper Hale and his family around, Father rarely takes pleasure in the simple joys.

Daniel rowed out to tell me he has been given one more week before he has to leave. I am so grateful.

Monday, September 16, 1861
P. Cloudy. Wind N.W. to N.E. Fresh.

Daniel and I pulled in a good number of crabs this morning before crossing the Ditch. The crabs fetched a fine price in town. I offered to give Daniel half but he refused. I gave the money to Grandmother, instead, to help pay Mother's expenses.

This afternoon Keeper Hale handed me a copy of Harriet Beecher Stowe's book *Uncle Tom's Cabin*. He said I may keep it.

Thursday, September 19, 1861
Clear. Wind N.E. Fresh.

Father left the station early again. He gives no explanation. I wish he would have waited and crossed with me on my way to school. Perhaps in the skiff he would have talked. Daniel always talks in the skiff.

Saturday, September 21, 1861
Fair. Wind S.E. Moderate.

Uncle Edward says the crop this year was abundant after all, in spite of the late spring. So there will be enough for soldier and civilian to eat. France and England, suffering from rains and ruined crops, and Ireland, with its blight on the potatoes, are eager to purchase the sum of our surplus agriculture. Their purchases will place needed money in President Lincoln's coffers.

Grandmother and Mother, with all that is going on around them, talked today only about the impertinence of shop girls. Mother's color rose with anger as she described the Negro girl behind the counter at the millinery shop. Mother was angry because the girl's dress was of a nicer cloth than she can afford.

A certain quality in Mother has been awakened by Grandmother. I am not certain I admire that quality, though I am grateful for what Grandmother has done.

Daniel's regiment left today for Maryland. He did not come to see me this morning. There was no time.

I stand this watch, knowing Daniel is gone. That I might never see him again. That is a hard and constant ache.

But I stand my watch.

Sunday, September 22, 1861
Cloudy. Wind N.W. Moderate.

Keeper Hale led us in prayer, a more sober and plaintive service than he has held for us before. Two hundred thousand men, women, and children in the single state of Tennessee have received notice to leave the state of their birth because of their Union sympathies. Those who own stores have been assaulted as they resist the theft of their goods by the rebel pirates. I fear for Uncle Edward in a town where he is surrounded by secessionist sympathizers, at a time when emotions are running so wild.

Daniel has been gone only a day and already I miss him sorely. Who may I confide my troubles to now? Not to Uncle Edward. He has troubles enough of his own. Not to Father. He is silent as the floor of the sea. Not to Keeper or Mrs. Hale. I do not wish them to think me unstable and therefore ill suited for my job. That leaves only you, my diary. And Napoleon.

Earlier today, I gathered the five little Hale children around me and read to them from the Bible. They were good and quiet for at least three minutes. And then they were off chasing Napoleon, who is allowed to come in the house these days. Now that Mother is not here.

Thursday, September 26, 1861
Fair. Wind S.W. Moderate.

The glass was broken in Uncle Edward's shop last night. And a fire set. I had a feeling something like this would happen.

When I saw what was done to my uncle's shop, I feared for his life. I raced through the open door.

There was Uncle Edward, perched behind his counter. The lingering smell of smoke stung my eyes. "We're fine, Wickie," he said. "Don't worry. Daisy and I extinguished the fire before it did any real damage."

Uncle Edward sat straight, his eyes glittering. Daisy had a bandaged hand.

"They won't drive me out," Uncle Edward said.

I thought about the people in Tennessee. They were being driven out.

Our Governor refused to proclaim today as a day of fasting and prayer for deliverance from our troubles, as President

Lincoln wished. The Mayor of Wilmington stepped forth and issued the proclamation instead.

The damage done to Uncle Edward's store was meant to send a clear message about how the people of Bayville feel about President Lincoln and his proclamation.

Now I am on watch. I try not to notice the burn of hunger in my stomach as the hours of my fast go beyond fourteen

I dozed off!

The alarm bell woke me, letting me know that the clockwork had run down. Immediately I attended to my duties. My heart pounding, I checked everything, everything from the Light to the oil reserves, from the inky night sea to the bell-buoy boat.

All is well. Nothing amiss. I am lucky. I am so lucky that nothing went wrong in the moments I slept. That the Light stayed lit, that no ship went aground.

If anything had gone wrong, it would have been my fault. Lost property, lost life, it would have been my fault.

Thursday, October 10, 1861
P. Cloudy. Wind N.E. Light.

I came softly upon Mother standing in Grandmother's garden this afternoon. I studied her before she was aware of my approach. She is so beautiful. Seeing her standing there, wrapped in her cloak, a bush of flaming red leaves behind her, it was easy to imagine how Father first fell in love with her. He used to tell me the story whenever I asked, about meeting Mother in Grandmother's garden, and knowing the moment he saw her that she would be his wife. . . .

The weather, up until yesterday, has been hot to the point of oppression, even with the ocean winds to cool us. The lantern room has been insufferable. But today it is cold, almost to freezing. And Daniel sleeps outside.

Thursday, October 17, 1861
P. Cloudy. Wind S.E. Moderate.

Uncle Edward has let me work in his store in exchange for a flannel undershirt for Daniel. It is easier to find an extra hour or two for Uncle Edward now that Mother is with Grandmother. Together the two are able to handle the sewing, the ironing and baking, all the light chores I had been doing for Grandmother myself. They only need me now for heavy chores, lifting and carrying.

I have tried to send a package or letter to Daniel every week. He writes back nearly as often.

I think of Daniel among the long lines of fires flickering and glowing in the night — all the tired soldiers, eating their suppers, settling into sleep while only the sentinels keep watch.

I am one of the sentinels.

Thursday, October 24, 1861
Clear. Wind N.W. Fresh.

Father woke me at dawn, at the conclusion of his watch. As I climbed the spiral stairs to the Light to begin morning chores, Father took the scow across the Ditch.

Please, I thought then, please, I have thought all day, do not let Father enlist in the army. Please do not let that be what he is doing when he leaves like this.

Perhaps I have lost Mother to her politics and her pain. Perhaps I have lost Daniel to his politics and the War. Must I lose Father, too?

There are things a father and daughter cannot discuss. But there are things a father and daughter must discuss. Tomorrow I will ask Father where he was today.

Friday, October 25, 1861
Clear. Wind N.E. Moderate.
Inspection at 4:45 P.M. Condition very good.

When I asked Father about his trip to the mainland, he grew angry. "Why can't you be a proper girl, Amelia? Why must you always question me?"

He might have tossed me over the balcony and dashed me to pieces on the ground below. But Keeper Hale came upon us and I pushed the hurt down deep where no one could find it. And that is where I shall keep it, as God is my witness.

Keeper Hale, Father, and I were briefed on precautionary measures during inspection today. We were told we must be vigilant throughout our watches for ships flying foreign flags.

There is a smell to the air on the mainland. Long ago I gathered chestnuts with William when the air smelled just this way. William will not gather chestnuts again. I would have liked to gather chestnuts with Daniel. Perhaps Daniel would have found my hurt and soothed it for me. But Daniel is not here. So I gather chestnuts alone. I once might have asked Reenie O'Connell to come with me, but Reenie will not speak to me now, because of her father. Is Reenie the proper kind of girl Father wishes me to be?

Thursday, October 31, 1861
Cloudy. Wind S.E. Moderate.

The frosty mornings of the past week have hastened my trips across the Ditch. I always row faster when I am cold.

I brought pumpkins back from Bayville as Mrs. Hale requested. Because the pumpkin crop is large this year, I was able to buy quite a few at a very good price. The skiff was so heavy with the enormous orange globes, it is a wonder I did not sink.

As I played with the Hale children, Mrs. Hale mixed a teacup of grated pumpkin, a pint of good milk, an egg, a little salt, two large spoons of sugar, some cinnamon, and some nutmeg. She lined a tin with pastry, filled the shell, and set the pie in the oven to bake. I asked if she would mind if I took some pumpkin to bake a pie or two of my own.

Mother loves pumpkin pie, almost as much as she loves peach. Father loves pumpkin pie, too. I am so angry at the two of them, tonight, after my watch, I shall bake two pumpkin pies and I shall eat them both myself.

Friday, November 1, 1861
Clear. Wind W. Fresh.

When I returned from Bayville today, Napoleon met me on the beach. He rubbed against my legs and mewed. Each time I started for the house, Napoleon ran toward the woods, then turned and ran back to me again.

I worried that perhaps one of the Hale children had gone to play in the woods and met with some mischief. But all five children were accounted for.

I threw myself at my house chores, for the dark comes quickly now and my shift at the Light comes early. When I headed to the Light at dusk, there was Napoleon, waiting for me, mewing, catching at my skirts and playing his game of running to the woods and back.

I had not time to go after him before my watch, but I promised myself I would follow him if he still waited when my watch ended.

Keeper Hale relieved me at nine and I had almost reached the house when Napoleon shot out of the darkness and yowled at me. Lifting the lantern, I followed him into the woods.

We had gone quite a way when I heard cursing, cursing such that I have heard only once before, and that from a sailor during a rescue. How he apologized for his language later when he found I was a girl.

I held my lantern aloft and continued toward the sound. To my astonishment I found Oda Lee Monkton leaning against a small tree. I knelt beside her and saw her face was bruised.

"What has happened?"

She stared at me, her face a mix of anger and pain.

"The girl looked white to me. Talked like she had money. I thought there might be some come my way if I helped her. Dang slave catchers caught me. The leg's hurt."

I did not understand anything but the last.

I fashioned a crutch for her from a green branch and with the crutch on one side and me on the other, we slowly made our way out of the woods to Oda Lee's.

I had never been inside Oda Lee's house. She was not happy to have me there now. Supplies were stacked everywhere. There was no place to walk, no place to sit, no place to lie down.

Oda Lee steered herself toward a pile of boxes.

The room was bitter cold.

I started a fire for her.

"I will row across and bring Dr. McCabe."

"Don't you dare."

She cursed at me and told me to get out. I stopped at the door, looked back at her. She was licking her hand and rubbing it over and over across a bruise on her cheek.

She screamed at me to leave.

Keeper Hale was still on second watch. I woke Father and told him about Oda Lee. I handed him the lantern and one of the pumpkin pies. He thanked me, sent me to bed, then left.

Oh, my diary, I don't know what to make of anything anymore.

Saturday, November 2, 1861
Fair. Wind N.W. High.

Father said Oda Lee helped an escaped slave last night and was beaten by the slave catchers as a reward.

I do not know what possessed Oda Lee Monkton to help a fugitive slave. But then I do not know what possessed her to help me last summer with the supplies for Keeper Hale's party, either.

Monday, November 4, 1861
Cloudy. Wind S.E. Fresh.

Father arrived at Grandmother's today while I was there. He stood in front of Mother and handed her a sheaf of papers. Mother took the papers, read down the first page, then shut herself in her room.

When after awhile Mother did not reappear, Father turned and left and I followed him. In silence I shadowed him across the Ditch, he in the rowboat, while I took the skiff. Once we had landed, I caught up with him and asked about the papers he had handed Mother.

Father kept his head down as he dragged his boat up out of the Ditch. He would not look me in the eye.

Oh, my diary, I think not knowing will drive me out of my mind.

Tuesday, November 5, 1861
Stormy. Wind S.E. High.

One of the highest tides I have seen in all my life. The marsh embankments have overflowed and fences have washed away. A number of houses along the Ditch are flooded by the invading tide. At least Mother and Grandmother are far enough inland that they are in no danger.

Father has checked on Oda Lee twice. She, too, is safe for the moment. He still says nothing about the papers, and I dare not row the Ditch today to see Mother and ask her myself.

Keeper Hale and his family have moved in upstairs with us until the storm and high tides run their course. We have given them Mother's room. Our quarters have never been so full of life. The children's sticky fingers and noisy activities are everywhere.

The sea has managed to get into the cistern. It was unavoidable, and now our water is salty. But the Lighthouse has weathered the storm so far, and though we lost our fence, the house remains undamaged and the Light continues to burn.

Here on the island, when a storm hits, nothing protects us from the mighty Atlantic. We have no barrier to buffer us the way we protect the mainland. We have only one another.

We must stand and take whatever the sea throws our way. And we do.

Mother could not.

But we do.

Thursday, November 7, 1861
Fair. Wind W. Moderate.

Mother was sleeping when I came. Grandmother said I was not to disturb her with any of my nosy questions.

Nosy questions!

I carried water and firewood in, but I did not do one lick of housework. Not one lick!

Thirty victims of the battle at Ball's Bluff were found Monday in the Potomac River near the Chain Bridge. They were much mutilated. No sooner did we have news that Daniel was at that very battle, fighting with the 71st Pennsylvania, but we had word he was one of the survivors. Daniel was not the only one to survive the fight. It seems the boys who were good swimmers managed to escape. I taught William to swim two years ago, after he nearly drowned. William must have taught Daniel. It makes me wonder why things happen as they do. I am filled with gratitude. I am filled with awe.

The beautiful Indian summer has come, with its soft and melancholy days. After the brush with winterlike weather, which set everyone to making provision for the coming frost and snow, the mild temperatures and balmy breezes have returned. This afternoon, the sunset blazed with a thousand hues.

Thursday, November 14, 1861
Cloudy. Wind S.E. Moderate.

A steamer wrecked on the shoals today. She was badly stove, with four feet of water in her hold. The Hale children wasted no time when I returned from school in describing to me in great detail how the steamer hit square and broke in two. Father and Keeper Hale took all aboard into the house and, because it was still early, delivered them across the Ditch, where they made their report. The insurance company will continue its interrogations here tomorrow.

The steamer struck in full daylight. Father and Keeper Hale saw her coming, saw there was nothing they could do to stop her. All that was left for them was to be ready for her. She was loaded with provisions. The cargo was strewn all along the shore. Oda Lee, still limping, has been busy all day. My guess is, she is still at it. She will be provisioned for a year on what she can take until an inspector arrives. I wonder where in those rooms she will stuff it all?

The army is now requesting woolen mittens, an article almost as useful to the soldiers as stockings. The mittens should be fashioned with a forefinger, otherwise they would be very unhandy in actual service.

I have found that cast-off woolen clothing, usually cut into carpet rags, is an excellent material for making mittens. I have been cutting mittens out from discarded cloth in every free moment I have had, and stitching them up in no time. I have finished three pair already. It is only want of material that keeps me from making more.

About 5,000 blankets for the army have been contributed by the people of the North. I have sent my own blanket along.

I sleep just as well in my cloak.

Thursday, November 21, 1861
P. Cloudy. Wind N.W. Fresh.

Daniel has written and asked for a likeness of me.

There are few more homely on the face of the earth. My ears are too big, my chin too small, and my cheeks always raw with the weather. I have never been one to dwell on appearance, a trait that has driven Mother and Grandmother to distraction. I do not intend to start dwelling on appearance now.

Daniel is a better friend than I imagined, to request a likeness of a face uncomely as mine. He says if he could look on my face each day it would bring him comfort. If having such a likeness brings him comfort, then I suppose I had better go to Frankford and have one made. But I would think such a thing would give him a start when he looked upon it. It certainly would me.

Thursday, November 28, 1861
Stormy. Wind S. High.

We had a fall of snow.

It gets dark so early now that we must kindle the Light in the afternoon and keep it burning well into the next morning.

Uncle Edward and I finally had a chance to talk yesterday. I have not had much time to spend with him. We caught up on events close to home. I asked after Daisy. She was away again, for a week. I asked if business had improved any. It had not. I did not mention the papers Father gave to Mother. It seemed disloyal to speak of them somehow. What do I know to speak of, anyway? Nothing! And besides, it was clear Uncle Edward wanted to talk about war. He said the rebel capital has been removed to Nashville, Tennessee.

Then he got onto the subject of slaves and cotton. He said the value of a field slave has always been measured by the price of cotton. When the price of cotton goes up, so does the price of a good field hand. When the price of cotton goes down, a field hand can be bought for a pittance.

With the blockade there is no way to ship out cotton, and no need for the slaves to grow more.

"Wickie, it is becoming a burden to be a slave owner. If we only persevere in our purpose for a year or two, no Southern man will be found rich enough nor foolish enough to wage war over the keeping of slaves."

I hope Daisy comes back soon. Uncle Edward seemed sore lonely yesterday with her gone.

Because of the weather, I was not able to cross the Ditch to see Mother on this day of Thanksgiving. After some consideration, I pulled on my storm clothes and ran to Oda Lee's shack and invited her to share the meal with us, but she chased me away.

I left a pumpkin pie on her step.

Keeper Hale led our prayer of thanks in the lantern room this afternoon. He said that all at sea on this day had taken their day mark from us, from the white column rising to the black tower topped by the lightning rod. He said all at sea this night would take their mark from our bright and steady flash.

We gathered at dusk for the lighting of the lamp.

Sarah and Alice entertained us in the tower, reciting a poem called "The Knitting of the Socks." I shall not forget the way Alice looked to Sarah with each line and the brightness of their eyes as they stood at the center of our attention. In that moment I understood the bond between loved ones. Why can it not be that way for my family?

I am standing my accustomed watch, first watch over the Light. Napoleon is here with me. Earlier, I fed him scraps from dinner and he licked the tips of my fingers.

I stroke his soft head and gaze out to sea, missing Daniel, missing Uncle Edward, missing Mother, missing the feeling of family after being with the boisterous Hales.

Wednesday, December 4, 1861
Stormy. Wind N.W. High.

December has come in raw and cold; the clouds are dark and threaten snow. Ice grips everything; the sides and decks of passing ships shine with an icy crust. The clapper on the bell has frozen again, and soon Father or Keeper Hale will go out to loosen it.

The conditions tonight are some of the worst. The windows of the Lighthouse rattle incessantly. They are encrusted with ice. I have come down again from scraping the glass surrounding the lantern room.

Just as I finished scraping this last time, I foolishly forgot to shield my eyes from the flash. In that moment of carelessness I was blinded. Suddenly I could see nothing as the wind tore at me. It howled and grasped at my cloak and my hood. I clung with desperate hands to the side of the Light. Such a wind, it fought to throw me from the balcony. I could not see at all. Blindly I crawled to the opening in the floor of the lantern balcony, groping for the top rung of the ladder. With the greatest care I struggled to make my way down to the safety of the watch room. As I descended, using only my numbed hands and feet to feel my way, the wind in all its fury plucked at me.

My legs and arms, my hands and feet, my face and ears are bitten through by ice and cold. But I am safe inside the watch room now and my sight has returned.

I must be more careful next time. The Light is not without pain. Life is not without pain. This I have learned.

As I sit here, my hands cramp with the cold and I struggle to hold my pen. I look at these hands, so miserable, so raw. I am humbled by the knowledge of the pain Mother must live with every day.

Friday, December 6, 1861
Clear. Wind S.W. Fresh.

Uncle Edward and I talked about the ending of slavery and the freeing of the Negro people. I have made it a practice never to speak politics at school. Everyone from the littlest Osbourne to the new teacher would turn from me. They all sympathize with the Southern states. I have yet to resign my position, but I grow increasingly unhappy at the school with each passing day.

This afternoon, Uncle Edward asked, how is slavery to be extinguished? By act of Congress? By edict of President Lincoln? How do you make a country stop such a habit, forsake such an institution? How do you legislate a people to give up not only its slaves, but the very concept of slavery?

Uncle Edward makes me think. While I am up here in the Light each night, I ponder his words of the day.

What he said today made me think of Father, when he was a captain. He could not discard all thought of winds and currents and intervening rocks and shoals, and simply steer by the North Star. Such a voyage could end in no other way but disaster. Nor can the Government simply declare an end to slavery and expect the country to sail safely through the shoals and rocks and currents along the way.

Nothing is simple, nothing is simply done.

Uncle Edward said, the real battleground of this rebellion is in *our* states, the border slave states. It is upon us that the burden of this War has fallen the heaviest. It is here that families are divided, that households are broken, that hearthstones are wet with blood and tears.

Father has become a ghost. He lives in the Lighthouse. He comes to our quarters only to eat or wash or change his stockings. I think he cannot stand the sound of the Hales any more than Mother could stand them, though I think their reasons are quite different. But in the end they are the same. Mother could not tolerate their joy, nor can Father. For one the sound is too much an imposition, for the other the sound is a reminder there is not imposition enough.

"I don't want Father to go to war," I told Uncle Edward today. Suddenly the words spilled out of me. I simply could not hold them inside anymore. And if I could not discuss the turmoil in my heart with Father, I had to discuss it with Uncle Edward. "Father has given Mother some kind of papers. I do not know what they mean. Either Father is going to war, or he is going to leave Mother and me. I do not want Father to leave. Not for war. Not for anything."

Uncle Edward held me close.

"Am I wrong to tell you this?"

Uncle Edward looked carefully down at me. His eyes were bright.

"No, Amelia," he said. "It's about time you did."

Thursday, December 12, 1861
P. Cloudy. Wind S.W. Moderate.

I weep at times here, when I am alone at the Light. I weep at times when I fall into bed at the end of a watch.

Tonight, an hour into my shift, while I was tracking a lumber ship, I heard footsteps on the spiral stair. I remembered when I heard footsteps and no one came. I thought it was a ghost then. Now I think it was Oda Lee.

I remembered when I heard footsteps on my birthday and it was Daniel.

I looked to the door, wondering who might be coming. It was a ghost this time. A ghost of a different sort. Father. Father surprised me, entering the lantern room.

I wiped at my cheeks but he could tell I had been crying. I busied myself checking the oil reserves.

Father put his hands on my shoulders and turned me to face him. We did not talk for a long time. So long that I am afraid the Lighthouse Board would have found me negligent had they been watching. And yet at the moment I did not think of the Lighthouse Board. I thought only of the weight in my heart.

As we stood there, so many thoughts went round in my head, like leaves in the wind. I could not catch hold of any of them and yet I knew them all. I knew them a hundred times too well.

Father led me down the ladder to the floor below. He guided me to the window and stood by my side, his arm around my shoulder. We looked out into the dark and blowing sea. In the flash, I saw a tall swell forming into a wave. Though darkness followed, I knew the story of that wave, how it would swell and curl and rush over the sand and through the grasses. Father and I both knew what that wave would do, even in the dark when we could not see it.

When the flash came again, the water was rushing back, back to the sea.

"I wish we could go back," I whispered.

Father nodded. He said he had been fighting against the tide. He was tired of fighting.

My hand tightened on the frigid sill. How cold it must be for Father to sleep here. How could he stand it?

Father said, "I spoke with Edward today. He said I have been selfish. He is right. I am sorry, Wickie. The papers. You should know. The papers I gave your mother. They are divorce papers."

I did not dare look at Father's face. Instead I studied his coat.

Father said he would take care of Mother as long as she lived.

"What will become of me?" I asked him.

Father asked what I wanted.

"I want to stay here, at the Light, always."

Father nodded, not to say I shall have what I want, simply to say he had heard me.

Thursday, December 19, 1861
Clear. Wind N. Fresh.

A letter from Daniel.

> *1st December 1861*
> *Near the Potomac*
>
> *Dear Amelia,*
>
> *With guard duty, picket duty, and a severe illness, your correspondent has been prevented from writing you for some time. If you will excuse the procrastination, he will endeavor to be more faithful in future.*
>
> *We have now every assurance of staying here all winter, and the prospect is anything but flattering. 'Tis bleak here — the wind howls dreadfully, and the white, heavy frosts of early morn warn us that winter is coming.*

We have picket duty in abundance, but we all rather like it. There is only one thing that mars our pleasure in service, and that is the cowardice of the rebels. If a few would only sneak up to us and get shot once in a while, it would ease the monotony that otherwise clings around us. Still we cannot blame them for their love of life, can we?

I will not deceive you. There is a great deal of sickness prevailing now in the regiment. The Doctor has had his hands full.

We have devotional singing and praying in one or more of the tents every night, and, as "Voice after voice catches up the strain," the effect is truly inspiring.

Your little packages are received with every demonstration of delight, and I take this opportunity of returning to you a soldier's thanks. I carry your likeness with me everywhere and often look to it for advice as I might look to you if you were near.

After next payday, which will be on the first of January, a furlough of ten days' duration will be given out, and one or two from each respective company given leave to travel home. Hope it shall be me.

Yours truly,
Daniel

Wednesday, December 25, 1861
Fair. Wind N.E. Light.

Christmas. It was an unusually quiet day. I went early to the mainland. Mother seemed strangely animated. But now it is late. Mother and Grandmother are alone by their hearth, Father and I alone, but for the boisterousness of Keeper Hale's brood. How grateful I am for their brightness. This morning Keeper Hale's youngsters found their stockings filled with goodies from Old Kriss — sugarplums, nuts, candies. I cannot imagine how Keeper Hale manages with so many mouths to feed, but he is not supporting his wife and her mother at a separate address, and Mrs. Hale, big-hearted as the sky, is most clever. She used tin patterns and baked fancy cakes for her family as well as for Father and me, and even one for Mother and Grandmother. At the noon meal together we untied the bag of chestnuts and ate the goose that we had kept and fed on corn.

Daniel is spending Christmas miles from home. Last Christmas I barely gave him a thought. This year is different. I look at the carving Father made for me last year, the carving of the Lighthouse. That little carving has brought me hours of comfort in this trying year. That and you, my diary. One of the aprons Mother sewed for me last Christmas I wore this

Christmas to bake cookies for the Hale children. Wearing the apron makes me feel that Mother is close by. And the drawing Reenie sketched hangs over my bed. Mother does not need it now. Not the way I need it, to hold her near.

I wonder what Christmas is like in the camps. Are the tents decorated with evergreens and colored lanterns? Do the ones receiving packages share with the others? Is there enough to go around?

Daniel, wherever you are, however you are, I wish you a merry Christmas.

Saturday, December 28, 1861
Clear. Wind N.W. High.

We are having a good deal of trouble with frozen feet in this terrible weather. Father bathes my feet in kerosene and rubs them every four hours, day and night. He does not let me do the same for him. He says his feet do not bother him.

Father feels guilty that I should have frosted feet. If I did not live in this buffeted Lighthouse station, if I did not work like a man beside Father and Keeper Hale, if I lived in the manner of a protected young lady, as Mother would have it, I would not have to concern myself with frozen feet.

But I have chosen this life. Frosted feet and all.

We are fighting a war of our own here. To keep the Light, in all weather, under every adversity. The other night when I struggled to keep the glass free of ice and Father struggled to restore the voice of the buoy bell, then we were soldiers in battle against the elements. Certain battles must be fought. I will fight to keep the Light. I will fight to keep Mother, too, in whatever way I can have her. I have lost something immeasurable in Mother's departure. But I have gained something immeasurable, too.

I read that some bachelors go to war because they like the fighting, some married men because they like the peace. I am not certain where Father falls within those lines of reason, but somehow, he has managed to find a peace of his own.

And I, though I have paid a price as dear as a lightkeeper's lifetime of wages, I, too, have found a certain peace.

I reread Uncle Edward's poem at the beginning of this diary and I understand.

Epilogue

Oda Lee Monkton continued looting ships until she died of cholera in 1866.

Keeper Robert Hale remained as Head Lightkeeper at the Fenwick Island Light until 1871, when he moved his entire family, except daughter Alice, to Alaska to accept a Government position.

After furthering his education, Edward Martin, Amelia's uncle, left Bayville in 1872 to teach at the newly founded University of Oregon in Eugene. Upon his death, in 1887, Edward Martin left all of his worldly possessions to his common-law wife, Daisy.

Mildred Martin, Amelia's mother, died in 1862, after suffering a seizure. Dr. McCabe ruled the cause of death as asphyxiation.

John Martin, Amelia's father, resigned as Assistant Keeper in 1863 after suffering a stroke. Alice Hale, Keeper Hale's second daughter, remained at Fenwick Island, looking after John Martin, from 1869, until his death in 1878. Alice Hale married Creighton Sydney of Ocean City, Maryland, in 1871, and she and Mr. Sidney brought great joy to John Martin's last years, surrounding him with their seven lively children.

Daniel Worthington survived the War and returned to Bayville and to Fenwick Island to marry Amelia in 1863. However, Daniel did not remain at the Light for long. Though they were never divorced, Amelia and Daniel lived only briefly together as husband and wife. Daniel went west, working as a supervisor on the Transcontinental Railroad. On the night of his death in December 1913, Daniel Worthington asked that a candle be lit in an old wooden carving of a lighthouse. The wooden carving was sent back to Amelia Martin along with a chest containing Daniel Worthington's personal effects and a rather large sum of money. The remainder of his estate was distributed between his two sisters.

Amelia Martin took over from her father as Assistant Lightkeeper at Fenwick Light in 1863, at the age of eighteen. She was appointed Head Keeper of the Ragged Island Light, a stag station off the Maine coast, in 1869, saving twenty-two lives over the course of her career as Head Keeper and receiving various commendations and awards, including the Medal of Honor. She retired from the Lighthouse Service in 1920. At the age of seventy-seven, Amelia began a new career, bringing books by boat to island residents up and down the Maine coast. Amelia Martin died in her sleep in 1940 at the age of ninety-five.

Life in America
in 1861

Historical Note

The tiny state of Delaware occupied an unusual position during the Civil War: It was officially a slave state, yet its citizens chose not to join the Confederacy. Instead, Delaware remained in the Union and fought with the North. Small as it was, the state lay on the border between North and South, between freedom and slavery, and those who lived there found room for disagreement and division among themselves.

The causes of the Civil War date to the founding of the United States, when Northern and Southern delegates to the Constitutional Convention disagreed over slavery. The framers of the Constitution compromised by writing about slavery without ever using the words *slavery* or *slaves* in their famous document. As a result, the first seventy years of the new nation were marked by continual tensions and negotiations between North and South, most notably on the question of whether or not slavery should be permitted in new territories and in new states admitted to the Union. As the North moved toward industrialization and wage labor, and the South developed as an agricultural society supported by staple crops and enslaved labor, the clashes between these vastly different economic systems grew more intense.

When Abraham Lincoln won the presidential election of 1860, Northerners were ecstatic, for they felt certain that Lincoln would prevent the Southern states from gaining more power in Congress. The white South, however, reacted to Lincoln's election with alarm because Lincoln believed that slavery should not spread beyond its present borders. Three months after the election, the seven states of the lower South voted to secede from the Union — to leave the United States. These states (South Carolina, Mississippi, Florida, Alabama, Georgia, Louisiana, and Texas) formed the Confederate States of America and elected Jefferson Davis as their own president. The Constitution of the Confederacy was similar to the Constitution of the United States, but with two significant differences: states' rights were strengthened, and the institution of slavery was recognized and protected.

At his inauguration in March 1861, Lincoln assured the white South that he would not attempt to end slavery in states where it was already legal. Although Lincoln personally judged slavery to be morally wrong, he did not believe it was his duty as president to impose those views on others. Lincoln did make clear, however, that the federal government would enforce the existing laws of the United States, which meant that the South did not have the constitutional right to secede, and the formation of the Confederacy was considered an act of treason. At the same time, because Lincoln's first resolve was to preserve the Union, he would not go so far as to declare war. In his inaugural address, he announced to white Southerners, "In *your* hands, my dissatisfied fellow countrymen, and not in *mine,* is the momentous issue of civil war. . . . You can have no conflict, without being yourselves the aggressors."

Fort Sumter, in the harbor of Charleston, South Carolina, belonged to the federal government. Lincoln had refused to surrender the fort to the Confederacy, for to do so would have condoned secession. But by early April, the United States soldiers stationed there were running out of supplies. Sumter would either have to be resupplied or evacuated. Lincoln made a careful plan, announcing that he would resupply Sumter with food only; there would be no resupplying of weapons, and the provisions would be carried on unarmed ships. These actions were intended to demonstrate that Lincoln refused to play the aggressor in a civil war that would tear the nation apart.

But the Confederacy interpreted Lincoln's plan as a declaration of war. On April 12, 1861, at 4:30 in the morning, the Confederates fired on Union ships that had arrived at Sumter. After thirty-three hours of bombardment, the federal government surrendered the fort, and the next day, President

Lincoln called up 75,000 soldiers from state militias to serve in the Union army for three months. Lincoln, and almost everyone else, felt sure that this would be a short military conflict.

In the spring of 1861, Virginia, Arkansas, North Carolina, and Tennessee seceded from the Union to join the Confederacy. White Southerners who owned the greatest numbers of slaves were the loudest supporters of secession and war. However, in the upper South, portions of the white population sympathized with the Union, notably in areas where the poor soil did not support the staple crops of a slave economy. Most white Southern Unionists lived in Delaware, Maryland, Missouri, and Kentucky. These were the "border states": slave states that bordered on free states and remained with the Union during the Civil War. The white populations of the border states were divided by the war.

Although Delaware permitted slavery, its economy shared more with the North than the South. Delaware farmers had always shipped their crops to northern markets on the Delaware River, and in the 1850s, the railroad solidified ties to Philadelphia and New York, while mills and factories were built in the Wilmington area. Wilmington had also served as an important stop on the "Underground Railroad," a network of black and white activists that provided food, shelter, and safety to fugitive slaves fleeing north to freedom.

By 1860, the vast majority of African Americans in Delaware were free, and a thousand black Delawareans joined the Union army. Delaware whites fought on the Union side ten to one. Still, many in the southern part of the state sympathized with the Confederacy. Tensions could run high within communities, and in each of the border states families found themselves on opposite sides of the war.

African Americans, in both the North and South, supported the Civil War as a means to create a nation without slavery. People who wished to abolish slavery called themselves "Abolitionists," and in the North, a minority of whites agreed that slavery was morally wrong and should not be tolerated anywhere in the United States. While Abolitionists were extremely critical of President Lincoln because they felt he wasn't doing enough to end slavery, the majority of Northerners supported Lincoln wholeheartedly. Most white Northerners backed a war to preserve the nation and were initially satisfied to restore the Union to a country half slave and half free. But that, too, would change as the war raged on.

The first major battle of the Civil War took place in Virginia in 1861. At the time it was fought, the First Battle of Bull Run was the largest battle ever in American history. The Confederate victory at Bull Run confirmed the confidence and righteousness of the white South. To the North, the defeat brought shock and fear. Finally realizing it would not be a short war after all, President Lincoln soon asked men to enlist in the Union army for terms of three years.

After Bull Run, the North worried that Confederates would invade Maryland, and Union soldiers stood guard on the north bank of the Potomac River. In October 1861, the Battle of Ball's Bluff, fought on the southern bank of the Potomac, ended in a dramatic Confederate victory. Although the year came to a close with considerable uncertainty in the North, 1862 would bring a number of important Union victories, most notably the Battle of Shiloh, the bloodiest battle in the entire western hemisphere at the time it was fought.

On both sides of the war, men who had enthusiastically signed up to fight — and had envisioned themselves returning home as war heroes — now experienced horrors on the battlefield such as they had never imagined. Those who survived witnessed death and destruction of tremendous magnitude and at close range, and many wrote home to tell their families what they had seen. Those on the home front suffered hardships as well, ranging from the daily miseries of food shortages to the overwhelming grief of losing loved ones.

As the second year of the war opened, it had become abundantly clear that neither side was going to surrender except in the face of total military defeat. Union soldiers now fought to destroy all enemy resources — and slavery was just such a resource. The goal of destroying the Confederacy therefore came to include the destruction of slavery. The Emancipation Proclamation, which Lincoln issued in 1863, forever changed the purpose of the war: All Northerners were now undeniably fighting to end slavery, and the official aims of the war now matched Lincoln's personal beliefs. The Proclamation also confirmed just how much the institution of slavery had already been weakened by the war. From the start, enslaved men, women, and children had seized the opportunity of wartime chaos to escape from their masters and run behind Union army lines. For slaves and their sympathizers, the Civil War had always been a war for freedom. Now that was official, too.

In 1861, very few Americans could have predicted that the Civil War would last four years and that 620,000 lives would be lost. In the course of those four years, North and South traded victories and defeats, but following General William Tecumseh Sherman's marches in 1864 and 1865, the Confederacy collapsed and surrendered in April 1865. The nation was united once again, but the bitterness of civil war would last for generations to come. In the United States, the institution of racial slavery had ended forever, but racial equality would prove to be a long way off, both in the North and in the South.

For years, mariners complained about the treacherous waters off the coast of Delaware known as the Fenwick Island shoal. Situated six miles east of Fenwick Island, this dangerous sand-bar caused many shipwrecks. In 1855, the newly established United States Lighthouse Board investigated complaints and deemed this area in need of a lighthouse to guide vessels safely to shore. Today, the lighthouse's appearance remains very similar to when it was first built.

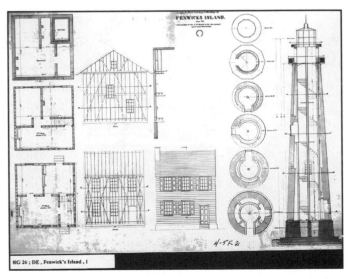

A blueprint of the Fenwick Island lighthouse details its unique construction: Two brick towers, instead of one, comprise the structure. The outer tower is conical, slanting inward as it ascends, and the inner tower is cylindrical. The interior and exterior tower walls measure seven inches thick and twenty-seven inches thick, respectively, making the lighthouse a secure fortress against even violent seas and storms.

The Fenwick Island lighthouse was first illuminated on August 1, 1859. The tower rises eighty-seven feet above ground, and its light is visible fifteen miles out to sea. Keepers and their families lived in the two-story house (right) located on the ocean side. The house's most unique feature is its cisterns, located in the basement. These concrete tanks are made to hold rainwater, collected through gutters, providing occupants with fresh, clean water for drinking and bathing.

The interior of this lighthouse emphasizes the proximity of the keeper's family quarters to the ocean. Girls' daily responsibilities in a lighthouse dwelling required the same chores—sweeping, scrubbing, and laundry—as did homes on the mainland. Whether working or relaxing, girls tied their hair back with ribbons and wore long skirts, usually sewn from fabric purchased at general stores.

161

1911 MONTH	DAY.	RECORD OF IMPORTANT EVENTS AT THE STATION, BAD WEATHER, ETC.			
January	1	Cloudy & Rain	Wind	S. E.	Fresh
"	2	Cloudy & Rain	Wind	S.	Fresh
"	3	Rain + Fog.	Wind	S. W.	Fresh
"	4	Clear	Wind	N. W.	Fresh
"	5	Clear	Wind	S. W.	Mod.
"	6	Clear	Wind	S.	mod.
"	7	Clear	Wind	S. E.	mod
"	8	Fair	Wind	S. E.	Fresh
"	9	Clear	Wind	N. W.	Gale
"	10	Clear	Wind	N. W.	mod
"	11	Fair	Wind	S. W.	mod
"	12	Cloudy	Wind	W.	mod.
"	13	Foggy	Wind	N. W.	Light
"	14	Cloudy + Fog	Wind	W. E.	Light
"	15	Cloudy + Rain	Wind	S. E.	mod.
"	16	Clear	Wind	N. W.	High
"	17	Cloudy	Wind	N. W.	mod
"	18	Cloudy + Snow	Wind	N. E.	Fresh
"	19	Clear	Wind	N. W.	mod.
"	20	Clear	Wind	N. E to S. E	Light
"	21	Cloudy	Wind	S.	Light
"	22	Rain	Wind	W.	Fresh
"	23	Clear	Wind	N. W.	Light
"	24	Clear	Wind	S. E.	mod
"	25	Clear	Wind	S. W.	Light
"	26	Cloudy + Rain	Wind	S. W.	Light
"	27	P. Cloudy	Wind	S. W.	Light
"	28	Clear	Wind	W. N. W.	Gale
"	29	Cloudy + Rain	Wind	S. W.	mod
"	30	Clear	Wind	W. N. W.	High

As shown in this 1911 log from Fenwick Island, keepers and their assistants continued to keep daily records of the weather the same way they did when the procedure began in the late 1850s.

162

In 1861, public schooling for children took place in small, one-room schoolhouses heated by wood-burning stoves. Teachers instructed all students in the same room, but provided varied lessons for different ages and abilities. Assistant teachers, usually former pupils, sometimes taught alongside them.

During the mid-1800s, ice skating was a favorite pastime among young girls and boys in cold northern climates. Skating took place on naturally frozen outdoor ponds, which put skaters at risk of falling through broken ice.

Abraham Lincoln was elected President of the United States in 1860. At the time there were well over three million slaves in the South. White Southerners did not want a President who opposed slavery, because their whole way of life—economic and social—depended on it. As a result, southern states seceded from the Union and formed their own government, known as the Confederate States of America.

In desperate attempts to evade their captors and escape to the free states, slaves used the Underground Railroad—a network of secret routes north. On January 1, 1863, President Lincoln's Emancipation Proclamation outlawed slavery and declared all slaves free. In actuality, however, this decree liberated few people because it did not apply to border states siding with the Union or to southern states already existing as part of the Confederacy.

Union boys' reasons for enlisting in the Army ranged from seeking change and adventure in their mundane lives, to preserving the Union, to abolishing slavery in the South. The minimum age requirement for boys was eighteen, but soldiers in the North and South were often as young as twelve. A typical Union soldier's uniform consisted of a navy four-button sack coat and navy wool pants.

A FAMILY QUARREL.

This 1861 cartoon expresses the conflicting political sentiments of families living in the border states. Dissension over the abolition of slavery was so widespread that even members of the same family fought about it.

The Smyrna Times.

ROBT. D. HOFFECKER, EDITOR.

SMYRNA, DEL,

THURSDAY APRIL 18, 1861.

Civil War--The Feeling Here.

The curtain has fallen upon the first act of the great tragedy of the age. Fort Sumter has fallen before the fury and prowess of a rebellion, and the " Stars and Stripes" of the great American Republic give place to the " Stars and Bars" of the Southern Confederacy. Civil War, that most horrible of all Wars, is now fully inaugurated. When it will end, God only knows. We have now the sad spectacle of a divided Country, broken confidence, prostration of business, and, instead of the busy hum of trade, we are greeted on every side with the noise of war and the resounding of the cry To Arms! To Arms!! The news of the bombardment of Sumter, though expected, was nevertheless received with a shock.— All hoped that something might yet be done to avert the desperate impending strife, but, as it had to come, the feeling seems to have been, let it come—anything but this dread suspense. We do not think the fall of Sumter produced any more, if as much, depression here as the passage of the ordinance of secession. Our peculiar situation in regard to locality has tended to counteract any decided feeling either way; but the last act of the drama commenced in November last has had the tendency to draw tighter and tighter the line of demarcation here as elsewhere, and the people are fast dividing for one side or the other. While there

The Smyrna Times, *a Delaware newspaper, announces the start of the Civil War following the Confederacy's attack on Fort Sumter, South Carolina—a United States military stronghold—on April 12, 1861.*

PUMPKIN PIE FILLING

Pare pumpkin, take out the seeds, and slowly boil until soft. Strain or rub it through a sieve or colander. Mix this with good milk till it is thick as batter; sweeten it with sugar to taste. Allow three eggs per quart of milk used. Beat the eggs well, add them to the pumpkin, and season with ginger and other spices to taste. Roll the paste rather thicker than for fruit pies, as there is only one crust. If the pie is large and deep it will require to bake an hour in a brisk oven.

Adapted from a mid-nineteenth century cookbook, this recipe details an old-fashioned method for making pumpkin pie. The crust, also homemade, would have been made separately.

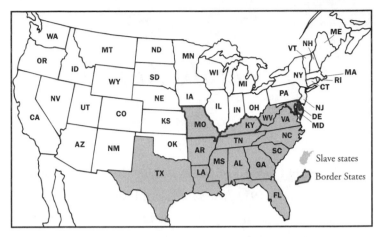

This modern map of the United States shows the slave states at the time of the Civil War.

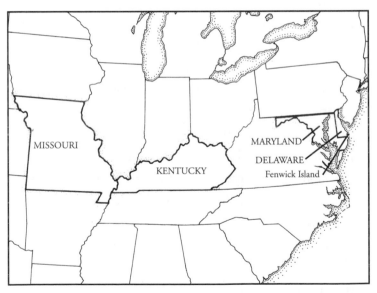

This detail of the four border states shows the approximate location of Fenwick Island, Delaware.

About the Author

KAREN HESSE says about writing this book, "While researching in the 1911 *New York Times,* I came across a series of articles written about Ida Lewis. Ida Lewis kept the Lime Rock Light burning off the coast of Newport, Rhode Island, during and after the Civil War, taking over her father's duties when he became too ill to serve. Ida Lewis never hesitated to go to sea in a storm, placing her own life in peril numerous times to rescue those who would otherwise have perished. She saved twenty-two people in her career as Lightkeeper. Yet she hated the attention her heroism brought. Ida Lewis saw herself as a Lightkeeper doing her job, nothing more, nothing less. Her story inspired me. To think of a female given such responsibility at that point in history! And the image of a light burning in the darkness of a Delaware night was so fitting when I looked at the darkness spreading over this country as the Civil War unfolded. Amelia Martin was created in Ida Lewis's image, and in the image of the other female Lightkeepers who sacrificed and struggled to keep their Lights burning through some of this country's darkest hours."

Karen Hesse is one of the most distinguished children's book authors in America today. Her acclaimed novels include *Out of the Dust,* winner of the 1998 Newbery Medal, the Scott O'Dell Award, and many other awards and honors; *The Music of Dolphins,* an ALA Best Book for Young Adults; and, most recently, *Just Juice.* She lives with her family in southern Vermont.

Acknowledgments

This book could not have been written without the assistance of Gladys Kennery, Wayne Wheeler of the U.S. Lighthouse Society, Paul Pepper, Tracy Mack, Jean Feiwel, Bernice Millman, Zoe Moffitt, Martha Hodes, Liza Ketchum, Bob and Tink MacLean, Eileen Christelow, Kate, Rachel, and Randy Hesse, Ken Black, Florence Thomson, Dr. John Straus, The State of Delaware Public Archives, The Library of Congress, Tim Harrison, Lorinda White, and Richard Shuldiner of the Brooks Memorial Library.

Grateful acknowledgment is made for permission to reprint the following:

Cover portrait: *The Umbrella* by Maria Konstantinova Bashkirtseva (1860–84). Oil on canvas, 1883. Collection of State Russian Museum, St. Petersburg, Russia. The Bridgeman Art Library International Ltd., New York, New York.

Cover background: *Desert Rock Lighthouse* by Thomas Doughty, 1847. Oil on canvas, 27 x 41 in. Gift of Mrs. Jennie E. Mead, 1939. Inv. #39.146 Collection of the Newark Museum, Newark, New Jersey. Art Resource, New York, New York.

Page 160 (top): Fenwick Island lighthouse, National Archives (RG Z6-LG-20-11)

(bottom): Fenwick Island lighthouse, blueprints, National Archives

Page 161 (top): Fenwick Island lighthouse and keeper's house, Delaware Public Archives, Hall of Records, Dover, Delaware
(bottom): Interior of lighthouse, Culver Pictures, New York, New York

Page 162: Weather journal of Fenwick Island lighthouse, National Archives

Page 163 (top): Schoolroom, Culver Pictures, New York, New York
(bottom): Ice skating, Brown Brothers, Sterling, Pennsylvania

Page 164 (top): Abraham Lincoln, Culver Pictures, New York, New York
(bottom): Slaves, Library of Congress

Page 165 (top): Union soldier, Library of Congress (LC B818410697)
(bottom): Civil War cartoon, New York Public Library Photograph Collection, New York, New York

Page 166 (top): *The Smyrna Times,* Delaware Public Archives
(bottom): Recipe for pumpkin pie filling, adapted from *Early American Cookery: "The Good Housekeeper"* by Sarah Josepha Hale, Dover Publications, Inc., New York, New York

Page 167: Maps by Heather Saunders

Other books in the Dear America series

A Journey to the New World
The Diary of Remember Patience Whipple
by Kathryn Lasky

The Winter of Red Snow
The Revolutionary War Diary of Abigail Jane Stewart
by Kristiana Gregory

When Will This Cruel War Be Over?
The Civil War Diary of Emma Simpson
by Barry Denenberg

A Picture of Freedom
The Diary of Clotee, a Slave Girl
by Patricia C. McKissack

Across the Wide and Lonesome Prairie
The Oregon Trail Diary of Hattie Campbell
by Kristiana Gregory

So Far from Home
The Diary of Mary Driscoll, an Irish Mill Girl
by Barry Denenberg

I Thought My Soul Would Rise and Fly
The Diary of Patsy, a Freed Girl
by Joyce Hansen

West to a Land of Plenty
The Diary of Teresa Angelino Viscardi
by Jim Murphy

Dreams in the Golden Country
The Diary of Zipporah Feldman, a Jewish Immigrant Girl
by Kathryn Lasky

A Line in the Sand
The Alamo Diary of Lucinda Lawrence
by Sherry Garland

Standing in the Light
The Captive Diary of Catharine Carey Logan
by Mary Pope Osborne

Voyage on the Great Titanic
The Diary of Margaret Ann Brady
by Ellen Emerson White

My Heart Is on the Ground
The Diary of Nannie Little Rose, a Sioux Girl
by Ann Rinaldi

The Great Railroad Race
The Diary of Libby West
by Kristiana Gregory

The Girl Who Chased Away Sorrow
The Diary of Sarah Nita, a Navajo Girl
by Ann Turner

This book is dedicated to all Lightkeepers — past, present,
and future — who kindle their lamps of hope against the darkness.

Copyright © 1999 by Karen Hesse

Library of Congress Cataloging-in-Publication Data
ISBN 0-590-56733-0
Hesse, Karen.
A light in the storm: the Civil War diary of Amelia Martin /
by Karen Hesse.
p. cm. — (Dear America)
Summary: In 1860 and 1861, while working in her father's lighthouse on an
island off the coast of Delaware, fifteen-year-old Amelia records in her diary
how the Civil War is beginning to devastate her divided state.
1. Delaware — History — Civil War, 1861–1865 — Juvenile fiction.
[1. Delaware — History — Civil War, 1861–1865 — Fiction.
2. United States — History — Civil War, 1861–1865 — Fiction.
3. Lighthouses — Fiction.   4. Islands — Fiction.   5. Slavery — Fiction.
6. Diaries — Fiction.]   I. Title.   II. Series.
PZ7.H4364Li 1999
[Fic] — dc21   98-49204
CIP AC

10 9 8 7 6 5 4 3 2 1   03 04 05 06 07

The display type was set in Garamond Semibold Italic
The text type was set in Garamond
Photo research by Zoe Moffitt and Pamela Heller
Book design by Elizabeth B. Parisi

Printed in the U.S.A.   23
First edition, September 1999

Reinforced Library Edition
ISBN 0-439-55535-3
November 2003